Angel Academy

Angel Academy

AARON M. STEPHENS, M.B.A.

UNITED AUTHORS PUBLISHING
THORNTON

ISBN paperback: 978-0-9908784-0-7
ISBN eBook: 978-0-9908784-1-4

Dedication

I DEDICATE THIS BOOK TO ALL THE
CHILDREN AROUND THE WORLD WHO LOVE
GOD/ALLAH.

Contents

Have you ever wondered about angels? Do they really exist? Where do they come from? Where do they hang out? What do they do? Are they always around us? Why don't we hear or see of them like people did in biblical times?

There is a magical realm where angels do exist. Angels are not seen in heaven, or found in hell. They are found on earth, in the skies, and another place known only to some as "Angel Academy". Here you will find angels of all sorts. They reside in this dimension to train, learn to become Warrior Angels, or hold some other angel occupation. Many angels are born because a soul loved another soul on earth so much that they sacrificed their heaven in order to watch over that soul and protect them. This is actually how new angels are born. Eventually these angels graduate to become Guardian angels.

This is a story about angels. This is not a new version of the angels the world already knows about. This is a story about new angels, and some old. There is no religious connection to any one faith, and it is the creation and manifestation of an earth angel telling a story.

@@*@*@*@

Note from the author: On several occasions, I have been visited by angels. They have filled my soul full of stories, pictures, and events, and given me the responsibility of creating a story for children and adults about angels. The world needs something to believe in. They need something magical. So it was God's intention to utilize me as a vehicle to create something fun and imaginative... something people could grasp onto, to know that there is something magical always watching over them. With that, readers also have to know that this does not make them invincible, and through the use of these stories everyone can grasp good and evil. It is my intention to share this version of what angels are like, and what secrets they hold; to paint life in a different shade of rose.

The world is ready to believe.

Preface

How did this book come to be?

Angel Academy is a collective works of stories, experiences, memories, and dreams that have come together in this book. I am so thankful that I allowed angels into my life. One day, in my meditation, I heard a voice, and I felt a feeling in my heart chakra that I cannot forget. It said to me, "The time has come for you to use the gifts you were given to tell God's message. *You*, Aaron Stephens, are an official scribe for God, and through this magnificent Opus Deorum, "Work of God", you will change the mindset and thinking of billions of souls."

At first, I thought it was pretty heavy. How was "I", who never wrote a story before in my life, going to be able to write something so important? I felt a hand on my shoulder, and I heard a voice say, "I will help you. You are the vessel. The message and story are already written."

Without looking up, I asked, "Thank you, my friend. May I ask your name, please? How long have you been here?"

The voice said, "My name is Malachi. I have been with you since you were born. I am your Guardian Angel. I am also a Herald for God, and I have been instructed by God to bare my presence to you, so you will once again believe in yourself and your abilities."

My eyes were filled with tears, despite them being closed.

"Why am I crying?" I asked.

Malachi replied, "A sign from God that you are a divine soul in the presence of angels; your eyes will display tears of joy and happiness. Revel in it and do not be ashamed."

All of the sudden, the feeling associated with tears of sadness, was gone, and instead a feeling of relief filled my heart. Malachi told me that I have the power to invoke angels at any time, and so when it is time for me to be the vessel, I faithfully declare:

A Writer's Invocation

"Lord, I thank you for the tidings and blessings of gifts you continually share with me. I thank you for sending me guidance with my dear angels. I welcome and invite any angel spirit or essence to use me as the vehicle to create the world's next masterpiece."

I light a candle and I close my eyes. I take a deep breath. When I open them, I am always amazed at what has manifested right in front of me.

I am divinely guided by angels. They have a message to tell the world.

The World Is Ready To Believe.

1

An Angel Is Born

Once upon a time, in a place far, far away, there lived a little angel named Braeden. He and thousands of other little angels all lived under one cloud, where they trained to be full-fledged angels which protect the souls on earth, help them fall in love, and defend the heavens from evil demons. This was a magical realm; a place of mystery, and for far too long it has been kept a secret. In ancient times, angels were talked about in the Bible and in stories, and lately, even in comic books. With their mighty wings and golden, glowing halos, they have captivated souls since the dawn of time. They represent goodness, light, and the word of God. They are non-denominational and love you regardless of what your soul may believe on earth. They usually appear young in age, and they are beautiful. It is easy to be captivated by their loving, glowing light.

A few angels actually graduate and are given the reward of being reborn on earth as Earth Angels. Someday, you may meet one, and one day, one may save your life. They are not easy to spot, but once one has touched your heart you have been provided a priceless gift, and you will never forget him or her. Earth Angels do not stay in one person's life for very long; they have work to be done seeking out troubles to fill with love and light. Earth Angels are the most loving creatures you will ever meet, as they have been touched by the very hand of God, and that love resides within their essence wherever they go.

Braeden is not an Earth Angel. He's barely an angel at all. Braeden just *woke up* as an angel and found himself at Angel Academy. Angel Academy doesn't exist in the earthly world. There is no way for humans to get there, or any other type of being for that matter. It exists on the spiritual plane right below heaven, above purgatory, and far out of touch from earth. Angels, however, can twinkle in and out from Angel Academy to heaven and to earth. They can even go to purgatory, other dimensions, and other scary places. Purgatory is a temporary place for souls that do not go to heaven.

Only angels exist in Angel Academy, although every few hundred years or so, Jesus has been known to stop by. Jesus spends *most* of his time in heaven, although it is a God-proven fact that he continues to go back and forth to and from earth. The word out on the street is that Jesus takes the form of a beautiful sunset everywhere that he visits on earth. Mortals can be heard saying out loud, "Oh, Jesus! Just beautiful!"

Almost all of the angels were created by God at the same time. At some point there weren't enough angels to go around, so God starting changing things around a bit. He sent out his Earth Angels to find worthy human souls, pure of heart, to be reborn as angels. Being selected to be reborn as an angel isn't like winning a prize or the lottery; it only happens when a soul does something that makes them *worthy*. Earth Angels select people because they have lived a life full of love, or continued to pay it forward, said, "please," and, "thank you," or gave up their seat on the train to an elderly person.

We may never really know what Braeden did to be

selected to become an angel; only God knows who Braeden really is. All we know right now is that Braeden lived on earth and he did a really great deed for mankind. He had a different mortal name, and he must have made an agreement with God to become an angel. He didn't remember his earth name, so Eugenia gave him a new one when he went through Admissions. It's also very possible that Braeden was not even a male on earth, but was actually female. If angels were allowed to swear, they would swear that Mother Theresa was somewhere in Angel Academy, but probably as a dude angel.

Witnessing a new angel being "born" is like witnessing one of God's greatest creations. In the Great Hall, trumpets start to blow, and angels from all over start to sing. Their voices are like beautiful harps. Looking up, one can only see blue skies and clouds, floating all around. There is no sun but there is light everywhere. At the center of the Great Hall is a circular room with a golden, glowing cradle surrounded by small little clouds. Hypnotic lights, glittering with gold and silver, explode with miniature fireworks. An angel is about to be born. With a little poof of gold dust, there sits the cutest, tiny baby angel. He is just so adorable. He would make someone think of the famous photographer, Anne Geddes, who photographed babies looking like little angels. He didn't have wings yet, but his energy field formed little baby wings on his shoulders. He blinked once, and then in a cloud of gold dust he went POOF and he was suddenly ten years older.

"Where am I?" he said.

He heard a voice reply, "Wait for it." And POOF, he was about four to five years older.

He stumbled out a, "Huh? What just happened?"

A female voice said, "Welcome to Angel Academy, my dear, little angel! You have gone through a birthing transformation. In a blink of two eyes, and in a cloud of magic Angel Dust, you went from infant to teen to... this."

He looked like a kid, barely old enough to drive a car. He was a little confused and he said, "What just happened? Where am I?"

Eugenia said, "Right this way, my darling, little angel. And by the way, your name is Braeden. You are a newly-born angel. We don't know the reason why you have been reborn, but we can only specu-late that you did something great on earth, died, and then God said that you could be an angel. So, here you are. Welcome to Angel Academy, the first step in your training."

He was naked, but he didn't seem to notice until Eugenia waved her hands and a silver and white tunic magically appeared on his brand-new angel body. The tunic was simple, yet ornate at the same time. There was a glimmering, braided edging around the arm openings and it was sleeveless, showing off his muscular arms. It was cut short and stopped toward the tops of his thighs. The back of the tunic showed his muscular back, and he wore a silver belt around his waist. He didn't have any wings yet, but the tunic was designed for a time when he would. On his feet were a pair of black and gold sandals. He stood about five foot eight inches tall, had blond hair, and would be considered stunningly attractive by mortals on earth. His perfect, white teeth matched his white tunic. He was, after all, an angel. He noticed that Eugenia and the other Admissions Angels were all wearing the same tunic.

Braeden tugged away and said, "Whoa, no one said I had to go through any training. And yeah, I am starting to remember a conversation like that."

Eugenia laughed and said, "Well, you can't just wish to be a full-fledged angel just like that. You will train here for a couple hundred years before you graduate. Come on now, you've already wasted twenty earth-years since you died. We don't have eternity."

Braeden seemed a little reluctant, but he made his way over to follow Eugenia. He wasn't sure why, but he couldn't remember anything about who he had been before he became an angel. He found out that he'd died, but why couldn't he remember his identity?

"You can stop wondering that right now, Braeden," said Eugenia.

"What?" he sputtered back.

She replied, "You were wondering who you were on earth." She raised an eyebrow.

"How did you know that?" he exclaimed.

"Well sweetie, while this isn't heaven, it's just like it only better. We communicate to each other through thoughts, and God communicates to us through feelings, which is the reason we radiate so much love with our presence. The moment you agreed to be an angel you also agreed to start fresh and new. So, your memory was wiped. Or as people from your time would say, it was deleted and reformatted."

Braeden asked, "Why would I have to give up my memory of who I was to be an angel?"

Eugenia said, "You chose to give it up; you only gave up your identity. You have almost all of your memories. The only thing you don't remember from who you were, was your name. Now you have one. It's Braeden. Lovely name. I made it up myself. One of the perks of my job."

Braeden looked around and saw that he wasn't the only one that had just been born. Other angels, boys and girls, were going through the same process that he was. Eugenia was only one of many Admissions Angels. While he stood there, he met Simone, Tonia, Alexis, Geraldine, Cecil, Hunter, and Maximus. Like himself, they were all confused. Each one was escorted by an Admissions Angel, and they left in a cloud of gold angel dust.

Eugenia didn't wait any longer. She had a lot of work to do, so with a blink of an eye she grabbed Braeden's hand and they "twinkled" out of the Great Hall into another glorious room.

2

Angel Dust

Angels get around the universe by "twinkling". Just like the stars twinkle in the sky at night, angels twinkle in a burst of beautiful, silently exploding colors that teleport the angels to wherever they want to go and leave glittery Angel Dust behind. If you look in the sky at night you can actually see angels twinkling from place to place.

New angels are born without wings and a halo, and do not know how to twinkle. Full-fledged angels have their wings and halo, and can twinkle quite easily. Like antlers on a deer or a goat, wings grow with age, time, or by exception. Exceptions include performing a good deed or saving a life. When angels are still training in Angel Academy it's kind of hard for them to grow their wings. Most angels get their wings when they are an apprentice. It is very common for an angel to twinkle in to a place with their wings and halo shining bright. For those who have witnessed an angel descending from the skies, it appears that a spotlight is shining down on the angel. It is a glorious and magnificent spectacle.

Some of the really ancient "celebrity" angels, like Gabriel and Michael, have the largest wings of all. Raphael once came to the Great Hall to announce the birth of a special child on earth, and his wings were each over a hundred feet wide, almost cloaking the room in the darkness of their shadows. Watching an angel expand or retract its wings is an amazing spectacle. It is almost like watching a peacock proudly display its feathered shield of beauty. Angel wings, of course, are not made of real feathers, but are instead made of energy that has taken the *shape* of feathers. Angel wings dissolve into white or gold Angel Dust and then disappear. Although humans cannot actually see the wings, some are sensitive to energy and can actually feel or sense them. Some have even reported hearing the sound of wings, like the sound of a bird taking off in flight. On some occasions an angel feather has been found and mistaken for the feather of a dove.

Angel Energy can take on any form that an angel chooses. An angel can instantly create a flaming sword or shield out of its own energy, and then quickly dissolve it to Angel Dust. Angels also have a magical and extremely powerful bow and arrow created out of Angel Energy. Each angel has a specific function, and some angels have multiple responsibilities. For example, a Guardian Angel cannot help a soul fall in love; only a Cupid Angel has the magical power to do that. There aren't as many Cupids as there are other kinds of angels. Cupids actually have to work a lot harder than any of the other angels, which is probably why no one wants to be a Cupid. Guardian Angels have the best job; all they have to do is "keep an eye on things," and even if they slip up, the slip up is blamed on the Angel of Death.

No one likes to mess with any of the Angels of Death. Guardian Angels and Warrior Angels have fought tirelessly against the Angels of Death. Sometimes they win, sometimes they lose. The battles are huge, and the outcomes depend on the willpower and faith of the human soul. When a human is on the edge of life, nearing death, such as in a hospital surgery, there is someone literally fighting to save that human soul. An epic battle ensues between good and evil on the astral plane. Warrior Angels typically do not interfere with the Angels of Death. Warrior Angels defend heaven. They are on earth to fight against the evil demons that hide among humans. Demons who try to do hurtful things do not survive when they come across these Warrior Angels. Some evil demons take the form of hurricanes, earthquakes, famines, and wars.

The Angels of Death are beautiful and scary... what is more beautiful than death itself? The Angels of Death usually appear as females who are kind and very trustworthy. Many of these angels are recognized for their somewhat "compassionate nature", and take souls who are in pain and are suffering; they are also known as Angels of Mercy. There are humans on earth who have also taken on that role, many of them being doctors or nurses, or workers in hospice. There are thousands of Angels of Death, as there are thousands of people that die every day. A lot of people picture the Angel of Death as a grim-reaper-type carrying a sickle and wearing a dark cloak, when actually they are quite gorgeous with glowing light surrounding them. Many times they will go to a dying person in the shape and form of someone that that person loved; the soul is more willing to leave its human form when it thinks that it is going with a loved one. A human may see one as someone standing in front of the sun, or in front of a bright light, and then in a flash they are gone. In a twinkle and a blink, an ordinary person watching would be left wondering if they imagined something, or if their eyes were playing tricks on them.

Watching a Guardian fight an Angel of Death is a rare event. Many times the fight begins as a civil conversation between two angels while sitting in a waiting room of a hospital, just talking it out. Then, one will walk out alone, and the other will be holding the hand of the soul. While you may imagine it as a bloody, gory battle to the end, it's really not. Angels don't bleed, and they usually don't die either. They *do* carry flaming swords that quickly scare away almost every evil entity. Esmeralda, an Angel of Death, took out an entire civilization back in ancient times with one Light Arrow; humanity experienced it as Mount Saint Helens erupting. Yes, the Angels of Death are certainly a power that one does not want to mess with. An interesting thing about Angels of Death, is that they are not "on" one side or the other. Sometimes when they take a soul, they don't take it to heaven. Instead they take it... down there. At Angel Academy they are called mercenaries... angels that didn't quite fit in at Angel Academy.

3

Angel Orientation

Braeden stood in the bright, white room and realized he wasn't alone. Eugenia dumped him off and she twinkled out of there, just as fast as she had twinkled in.

"Wow, when am I going to learn how to do that?" he said out loud, not paying attention to anyone around him.

A soft female voice replied back, "Oh, you'll learn that easily in the first ten years or so."

Braeden turned to the soft, pretty voice and saw another wingless, halo-less angel sitting next to him. At that point he realized that they were both wearing a silvery, glowing, white tunic and that they were also both wearing gold sandals. For the first time, he realized he didn't even know what he looked like.

"Hi, I'm Braeden. I was born just a few minutes ago."

The pretty angel politely said, "Actually, Braeden, you've already been here for ten earth-years. Time works differently here. I'm Morgan, by the way."

Morgan was really pretty. She had long, white hair that went past her shoulders and she looked like she was only twelve or thirteen years old.

Braeden replied back, "Wow, time really *does* fly when you're having fun! I'm still kind of new here. I haven't even seen what I look like. I don't see any mirrors anywhere."

Morgan giggled like a little schoolgirl and said, "You're funny. All angels are young and beautiful. You are quite the looker." She held out her hand and blinked, and a cloud of gold glitter smoke magically appeared. A gold, handheld mirror manifested. She held it out and said, "Here ya go, hottie!"

Braeden took the mirror and stared at it for thirty seconds. This was the face he had always wanted. He was attractive, even hot! He looked so young. He wished he could remember what he had looked like as a mortal, but he knew that it hadn't been anything like this.

Braeden handed the mirror back to Morgan and was about to ask another question, but then he remembered what Eugenia had said... *telepathy*. So instead, he "thought" to Morgan, *"How long have you been an angel?"*

Her eyes got big and she said out loud, "I have been an angel since the dawn of time. I see that you figured out thought transmission. Soon you will learn about our other communication methods. Right now you can only hear what you can see, which is me. Soon you will learn about Angel Radio and Angel Technology." Braeden was just amazed. This was the coolest thing that he had ever seen. He was still fairly young, unlike Morgan who was older than old.

"I am just wondering, if I am a new angel, and you are an... uh,... old angel, what are you doing here with me?" thought Braeden.

Morgan replied out loud, "You are my apprentice. You will be with me at all times, or supervised by a Senior Angel, and I will train you on how to be an angel. For the first hundred years or so, your powers are limited only by what I allow. There will be no flaming swords or Light Arrows for you for at least three hundred years."

Braeden asked out loud, "So, when do I get to be on my own so that I can go protect my family?"

Morgan looked him straight in the eyes and said, "You think you are going to remember your family when you don't even know *who* you were? My dear little padawan, by the time you learn how and what you need to do, your family, *if* you remembered them, will have long ago died and gone to heaven. You were granted your one true wish when you talked with God. It was, 'I wish that I could be an angel so I could protect my family.' God said, 'Wish granted,' and you were immediately transported and re-birthed here. The one thing that no one ever knows or is told before coming here, is that time works differently here. In what seems like an instant here, weeks have passed on earth. A week here, and a month has gone by there. A month here, and an entire civilization on earth has crumbled. A year here, and man has evolved and started to destroy the beautiful gifts that they were given. You can only protect your children's children."

Braeden didn't think this was fair. He felt cheated by God.

Morgan said, "You weren't cheated by God, you were granted your one true wish. You should be eternally grateful, as not every soul on earth can just *be* an angel. If you would have just died like a normal person, then you could have easily watched over and protected your immediate family from heaven. But you had to go and say, 'I wish I was an angel,' and God said, 'Granted.'"

Braeden realized that she was right, and that God was right, and it was his own doing that put him where he was now. He asked Morgan, "What if I change my mind and just want to go to heaven as a regular person?"

Morgan smiled and said, "Oh, you will go to heaven all right, just not as a mortal soul. Now stop obsessing over it. You are an angel now and there's nothing that is going to change that."

Braeden still wasn't totally convinced and continued to ask more questions. "What if an angel decides at some point not to..."

Morgan interrupted him before he could finish and

yelled, "THERE IS NO DISOBEYING GOD AND THERE IS NO GOING BACK." Her wings and halo exploded in a flash of white light. Her eyes turned bright white, and more light poured out of the place where her eyes used to be. It was beautiful and also very terrifying. She didn't have any weapons, but she didn't need any as her gigantic wings and halo were engulfed in white flames and her halo burned so bright that Braeden could barely stand to look at it. He could see how Morgan could very easily be a figure of fear. She touched his forehead with her index finger and he instantly saw flashes of war, terror, battles, and finally what appeared to be an angel. It wasn't a young and beautiful angel, but an old and decrepit one. Its wings were featherless and its skin was gray. It had long, black, oily hair and where the feathers should have been was instead a translucent, see-through skin. Its face was mangled and deformed, and it looked awful. He saw Morgan fighting this "thing" with her sword, arrows, and all of her might. She was a force to be feared. She slashed, tore, and destroyed what used to be an angel. Hundreds of these flashes of images poured into Braeden's mind, and he immediately knew the utter destruction that an angel could dish out. He wondered who that angel had been and what had happened to him.

Just as quickly as Morgan had erupted, she instantly became the same beautiful, peaceful angel as before. Her wings exploded into silent, gold fireworks, and Angel Dust littered the floor. She smiled politely and said, "Any questions?"

Braeden sputtered out, "THAT!!! THAT thing was an angel? What happened to him?"

4

Talking To God

"I knew you would have that sort of a reaction upon seeing what a not-so-happy angel looks like," said Morgan. She seemed pretty pleased with herself. Braeden decided this was something that she must do to all the new angels.

Braeden stood there and asked the same question again, "Was that really an angel? What happened to him?"

Morgan obviously knew that this topic of discussion was going to come up when she brought out the halo and the wings. You don't get all "holier than thou" and then just drop it. She said, "Well, I don't know who you were on earth before you were an angel, so I have no idea what you believed, read, or saw in movies. But, I do know this... there are all kinds of versions of what people think God and angels are like, and what they aren't like. For the first few hundred years of your angel life you are going to learn a lot of things. Some of the things you may like, some of the things you may not like. You will bear witness to some of history's tragedies and learn who, what, and why things happened the way that they did. You will exist in a reality that is nothing like anything you have ever experienced. We, as angels, do not follow or believe in only one religion. Humans make their own societies, and within them they create what they think heaven is, and for some religions, hell. What happened to that angel was the result of some bad choices. I'm not going to lie to you, Braeden, there are a lot of evil entities out there. Those scary stories about demons are not just stories. That one that you just saw me destroy? It was seduced by a demon and... well, you saw the consequence."

Morgan took him by the hand and started to lead him out of the large, empty, white hall. After a few minutes he realized that he was actually floating, not walking, down the hall. "When do I get my wings so that I can fly?" he asked Morgan.

She replied, "Well, my little angel, you have a lot to learn before you get your wings. Technically, you can fly now. Wings are actually the manifestation of your ability to control your Angel Dust. It is the source of your power and you can create anything simply by thinking of it. You will learn it soon, but first you will need to decide on an angel occupation so that you know what it is you will be creating. You do not have a sense of time here, so it is difficult to say when it will be, but soon."

Things started to make sense for him. The more that he held onto Morgan's hand the more he could feel her energy, and with it, a clearer understanding.

"Where are we going?" he asked her softly.

"I am taking you to your history lesson and education. There, you will learn everything that you need to know about being an angel. All of your questions will be answered very soon."

He squeezed her hand and said, "And when do I get to see and talk with God?"

She replied, "You already spoke with God when you died and chose to become an angel. If you are wondering when you will hear from God again, the answer is very soon. Although you don't think that God is paying attention, God *is* all, and knows every-thing. There is no escaping God when you are in Angel Academy. You can't hear it yet, but God is constantly talking to angels, simultaneously having conversions with billions and billions of souls and angels all at the same time. It's pretty amazing. One thing is pretty unanimous across all religions, and it is that humans know they can't order or tell an angel what to do, even their own Guardian Angel. All humans go through Jesus or God to ask God to send help or whatever."

Suddenly there was a flash of bright light, and she and Braeden twinkled out of the long hallway into yet another amazing room. This one was nothing at all like the last two places that he had seen, and instead of white everywhere, it was lush and green. Palm trees and a water oasis surrounded him. It was a tropical paradise, and yet, there was still no sun.

"Where are we?" he asked.

A new, male voice from behind him said, "You are in the entryway into the library. It's pretty amazing, isn't it? My name is Taylor and I'll be teaching you some of the basics. Morgan tells me she has some assignments on earth to tend to, and she will be back shortly."

Taylor was another beautiful, young-looking angel. He had light brown hair, cut really short. Braeden couldn't see his halo, but he could see the glow that it emitted which surrounded his entire body in a soft, white light. He also wore a similar tunic to Braeden's, but he had a little gold badge on his that said "Taylor, Senior Angel" engraved in black lettering. Braeden looked at it and wondered if it meant that he was an old angel like Morgan.

Taylor laughed, smiled at Braeden, and said, "No, it doesn't mean I am old. It means I am in charge of an area. In this case, it is the library. There is a hierarchy in Angel Academy, and you will know it soon enough."

Taylor took his hand and they floated across the beautiful, blue waters through the trees until they came to a gold door with a symbol on it. The symbol consisted of wings and a blazing oval in the center of it, like a halo, and underneath it were the letters "AA". It was the official insignia for Angel Academy. Taylor put his hand on it and it opened, uncovering yet another spectacular room.

"Is this the only way into the library?" asked Braeden.

Taylor said, "Only if you don't know how to twinkle, which is why we are going this way."

Braeden liked the energy he felt from holding Taylor's hand. It had a different feeling than holding Morgan's hand; a vibration and almost a tingle. Braeden wanted to know why it felt different.

Before he could ask the question Taylor said, "The feeling you experience interfacing with me versus Morgan is different because I am the official keeper of knowledge for the heavens, and because of my position, I'm closer to God than Morgan is. When *you* get even closer to God, you will know the feeling immediately."

Braeden was just amazed at what he saw when he walked into the "library". It was funny that they called it a library because he couldn't see any books. For the first time he thought that he saw other angels, but they didn't *look* like angels. From where he was standing, he could only see little balls of light zipping across the skies.

"What are those silver balls of light?" asked Braeden.

"Those orbs of light are angels, just like you. They are more.... experienced, and can transform into those little balls of light to get to places quicker. In order to enter into any of the library's documents, you have to be a ball of light," Taylor replied.

"While you may know a library on earth as being a place that holds books, here in Angel Academy, and in heaven, "library" has a very different meaning. All of the historical "documents" are in these halls, stored as experiences, and contained in magical portal dimensions. Here, you can step into the experience of anything that happened in time. While you are inside of a historical experience as an angel, humans cannot see you, nor can any of God's other creations. If there are other angels there at the same time, you can talk with them. You will also be able to hear exactly what God had said to the angels at that time, and what he had said to any humans. You can observe, witness, take notes, hear a soul's thoughts, and listen to their words, but you cannot interfere or change anything that happened there. There are *some* angelic, enlightened individuals on earth who know about the library, but they call it the "Akashic Records", or the "Hall of Records". Every known thing in the universe is documented in the library. I will introduce you to Desiree, the Senior

Angel of Mythical Creatures. New angels always love that experience. And yes, unicorns and fairies are real."

Braeden asked, "So, are you telling me that every single event that ever happened on earth is recorded here, in this library? And if I want to go visit and experience something, I can do it here?"

Taylor nodded yes.

Then Braeden asked, "How do I become a ball of light, and are there any limitations to what I can or can't see?"

Taylor waved his hand in the air and a cloud of gold Angel Dust appeared. In it, he saw a lovely face of a female angel. Her white hair was pulled up in an elegant hairdo. She had perfect, creamy white skin, and was the most beautiful angel that Braeden had seen. She, too, had a glowing, golden aura emanating from her halo.

The angel turned to Taylor, smiled, and said "What a nice surprise, hearing from a Senior Angel. What can I do for you, Taylor?"

Taylor flashed a huge grin back and said, "Well, if it isn't my favorite Angel of Light. Hello, Aleona,

I'd like you to meet my newest recruit, Braeden. He was just asking about balls of light and I thought it would be best if my favorite Angel of Light were here. Would you mind joining us in the library?"

Aleona replied, "Of course, Taylor. I am having a conversation with Father right now, but I will be there in just a moment."

The cloud of gold Angel Dust magically dissolved, and in less than a second Aleona twinkled into the library and was standing in front of the youngest angel. She appeared with her wings fully spread and her halo shining brightly. Braeden noticed that her Angel Energy was much different than Morgan's or Taylor's. It was hypnotic.

In person, Aleona was far beyond beautiful. She was... enchanting. Braeden couldn't stop staring at her. She constantly radiated a glowing light that almost pulsed. It sparkled and glittered, and left Angel Dust everywhere. She wasn't wearing the same kind of tunic that Braeden and Taylor had on. Instead, she wore an amazing, white, silvery gown that almost floated around her. She had on a see-through type of shawl that wrapped around her right shoulder and floated around her body and gently next to her gown, all without touching it.

Retracting her gigantic wings, she floated over to Braeden. He noticed that her halo remained on, glowing brightly. Braeden wasn't sure how to address this Angel of Light, so he got on one knee, bowing to the beautiful angel named Aleona.

She smiled and gently laughed. "My dear, little angel, there is no bowing to me or any other angel. We are all equal. Yes, there *is* a hierarchy, but we are still all equal." She leaned over and gently kissed Braeden on the forehead, leaving a very tiny, little mark. If you looked really closely, you would see what looked almost like a snowflake.

"I have just given you the ability to turn into a ball of light, as you call it."

At first, Braeden didn't feel any different than he had felt before Aleona kissed him, but then suddenly he felt a little tingle in his heart and in his forehead. He wasn't sure what was going to happen next so he said, "Thank you, Aleona. I am honored to meet you."

She replied with a beautiful smile, "You are *ever* so welcome," and took Braeden's hand in her left hand, and Taylor's hand in her right. "I know exactly where you want to go first, so let's get it out of the way. I will help you the first few times."

Braeden looked over at Aleona and Taylor, and asked, "Are you sure you know where I want to go and what I want to see?"

She and Taylor both smiled. Aleona replied, "You are going where every new angel goes during their first decade of existence. You are going to see the birth of baby Jesus."

She and Taylor looked at each other, and said at the same time, "God love me." A poof of gold dust exploded around them, and they were instantly transformed into three balls of light, zipping up to the center of the room and crashing into the moment of "Baby Jesus's Birthday."

5

Happy Birthday, Baby Jesus

Being a ball of light was very different. It wasn't anything like twinkling. Braeden and his new angel friends were tiny, miniature balls of silver-white light also known as "orbs". It felt almost like he was in a magical, spherical spaceship. He liked this feeling. He was flying without any wings.

He thought to himself, *"This is amazing! I love this! Can I do this anytime I want?"*

Aleona thought back to him, *"Yes, you can become a ball of light and fly anytime you want. All you have to do is concentrate and say, 'God love me.' To return to angel form, simply think, 'Jesus love me'."*

In an instant, the three of them landed on the floor of a straw-littered barn. As soon as they touched down, at the same time the three of them said, "Jesus love me," and then were instantly inside of a cloud of gold Angel Dust within a very, very crowded manger. Not only were there humans there from across all of the lands, but there were also thousands of angels all standing by, watching, hovering, floating, and flying all over. Braeden glanced outside of the barn doors and the skies were filled with angels... hundreds, no, *thousands* of angels were everywhere. He looked directly above where he was standing and he saw a very bright star. It was the brightest in the sky, and it lit up the land for miles.

Aleona said, "The mortals call this the Star of Bethlehem, as this is where the barn resides. It is not actually a star. It is the Great Hall within Angel Academy where you were born, which is directly below heaven. Mortals think that the star shone brightly in order for the humans to make their way to the birthplace. Before Jesus was born, for forty days and forty nights there were no baby angels born, and the Great Hall remained silent and dark. This was the only time, ever in history, that the Great Hall shone so brightly after being dark for so long."

Taylor and Aleona were still holding Braeden's hand. Taylor looked over and thought to him, *"Remember, Braeden, this is a historical experience and every angel that has ever come to witness this has been recorded. Your visit today will also be recorded. Don't be nervous; Father is coming soon, and the baby Jesus, too. You will be filled with his love and glory. You will also have the privilege of seeing Marcia, the Angel of True Love. She is the Senior Angel over Cupids. She will bless the baby and gift him with True Love."*

Braeden stood there, anxiously awaiting the arrival of the three holy spirits. All of the sudden, the room filled with a warm, glowing light. It was so bright that Braeden had to look down and away from the Virgin Mary. Then, his heart filled with a warm sensation that he had never felt before.

Braeden looked over at Taylor, and Taylor thought to him, *"It is time; our Father is here. You can feel his love."*

A minute later, the baby Jesus arrived, and just moments after, Marcia, the Angel of True Love, twinkled into the barn. Taylor explained that she had actually been there at the time of the arrival, hence seeing a twinkle instead of a ball of light. Braeden looked over to the left of the stable and saw Taylor, Morgan, and Aleona in the crowd of angels. They, too, had been there, but he was only seeing them in the past.

If Braeden had thought that Aleona was beautiful, he was absolutely mesmerized by Marcia. Although Marcia only looked like she was twenty years old, Braeden knew better. She had soft, light hair, swept up into a very elegant hairstyle. Braeden wondered just how long her golden hair actually was when it wasn't pulled up. She wasn't wearing a silver tunic uniform, but instead proudly displayed an extremely angelic, silver ball gown that she wore with silver gloves up to her elbows. In her hair she wore little crystal hearts that were actually hairpins that made her hair sparkle. Her gown was similar to Aleona's in how it floated around her. She, too, was wearing a gold nametag like Taylor's, and hers also said "Senior Angel" on it. The one thing that was different was that there was a little, red, ruby heart on hers. Marcia also wore tiny, red, ruby hearts as earrings, and had a diamond charm bracelet on her right wrist. The bracelet sparkled with a bright red, ruby heart that appeared to dangle, or possibly just float next to her wrist. On her other wrist, Braeden noticed that she was wearing a similar gold bracelet that matched her nametag. It was only then that Braeden noticed that *he* didn't have a gold bracelet *or* a nametag. All of the sudden he wanted his own.

He looked over at Taylor, and Taylor thought to him, "*The bracelet will be given to you later at your coronation ceremony. The nametag comes with a promotion.*"

Braeden was happy with that answer and he continued to be entranced by Marcia.

Aleona squeezed Braeden's hand, and thought, "*You will meet Marcia soon. This is just a memory. It's not really real.*"

Braeden was really excited to hear that. He really wanted to touch Marcia's hand to see what he felt. He knew for certain that True Love was going to feel a lot different. Braeden watched Marcia lean down, kiss the baby on the forehead, and then leave as quickly as she had come.

While this was going on, Braeden noticed that the human mortals were extremely excited, and mortals from all over were coming to bring gifts to the baby. Braeden already knew this part of the story, and he was more interested in the angels that surrounded the baby Jesus. Braeden was just amazed at what he saw. He saw every possible kind of angel around... he'd had no idea that it had been such a huge ordeal, with angels and all. This was the only day that every angel in the universe had been in the same place at the same time. He looked around, and angels were whispering and talking amongst themselves.

Aleona squeezed Braeden's hand and looked over at him. "Are you ready to go back?"

He nodded yes, and the three of them said, all at once, "God love me." In a flash of light and a poof of gold dust the three of them were all little balls of light again.

"Where to now?" asked Braeden.

Taylor said, "Onward and upward, as we take you to your next exciting experience. We're going to heaven!"

6

For Heaven's Sake

This was it! He was finally going to heaven to see it for himself. He would be able to see his dead friends. Braeden could barely contain his excitement. Then he realized, he didn't *have* any dead friends. With a poof of gold dust they magically touched down, and the three of them all said, "Jesus love me." He saw three innocent angels standing on a cloud. Braeden looked around, and it looked a lot like Angel Academy.

"I thought we were going to heaven," said Braeden.

Braeden heard a very familiar, female voice reply

back, "Heaven looks different to us than it does to the human soul. For starters, you can't see any human souls and they can't see you."

Braeden turned and saw the lovely Morgan standing there, radiant as ever. She was no longer wearing a simple tunic. Now she was wearing a beautiful, long, silvery-white, glowing gown that covered her feet. Her long hair was pinned up and she looked very sophisticated. She looked like she was going to a really formal event. She didn't have a nametag on, but Braeden noticed Morgan's gold bracelet which was identical to Taylor's and Marcia's.

She smiled at him and said, "Thank you. I do try to impress when I am in heaven. Don't I just look divine?"

Braeden nodded in agreement; she looked amazing. Braeden didn't like that he couldn't see human souls. He was hoping to see some dead people that he used to know, or at least a celebrity.

"Morgan, why can't we see human souls?" he asked.

"Well, for starters," she replied, "it would violate one of the Angel Laws. We are not allowed to interfere with human souls. Heaven isn't for us, it is for them.

We have Angel Academy, and they have heaven. It's called a different name, but look around. Doesn't it look just the same?"

Braeden had to agree, things looked just the same.

Morgan thought to Braeden, *"Angel Law. Under no circumstances are humans allowed to see angels. Also, angels are not allowed to time-travel to a prior human existence, not that you would ever find out who you were."*

Evidently, that meant on earth *and* in heaven, Braeden thought to himself. He thought it was kind of strange that humans didn't see angels. He thought that contradicted things he had remembered from his time on earth, but the more that he thought about it, there really hadn't been any real angel sightings since the Bible had been written, so maybe it was a new law that had been passed.

Morgan heard what he was thinking and said, "You are absolutely right. God made a law a long time ago that angels were not to be seen or heard by human mortals. However, there are a few individuals on earth who have communicated with angels, and have *maybe* even seen them. Humans are more secretive in their angel sightings, and most of the time do not share these events with each other. Some angels, like Heralds, are exempt from that law. Michael and Gabriel are Heralds. As a precautionary measure, the "Tear Act" was instituted, which causes human mortals to start crying in the presence of angels in order to make it harder for them to see us. They have an awful time seeing anything when their eyes are covered in tears."

As quickly as it had come into his thoughts, it was gone just as fast. He was *in heaven,* and he was finally going to talk with God. Surely there was more to heaven than what he was seeing.

Morgan interrupted his thinking and said, "Yes, you are correct, there is more to heaven than just this. Just like in Angel Academy, this room is just a passageway into another great, divine hall. As angels, all we see is the reflection of Angel Academy. It's designed that way so that everyone feels at home in their own heaven."

Things were quickly starting to make sense to Braeden, and he was liking every minute of it. They floated along the gigantic, white columns that lined the grand hallway. Although this was just a passageway into another room, it was grandiose, opulent, and impressive. As the four angels floated together, Braeden began to ask more questions.

"Taylor, are angels here all of the time and humans can't ever see them? What about the pearly gates that human souls supposedly go through to get to heaven?"

There was a chuckle among everyone, and Taylor said, "Do you see any gates?"

Braeden looked around and said, "Nope."

Taylor said, "Yeah, me neither. So whoever told you that there were gates must have been confused The only way you can get into heaven is by twinkling in. A lot of the Angels of Death complain that they are nothing but fancy taxi-cab drivers. The truth of the matter is, entities have been trying to get into heaven for ages. There are a lot of lost souls that never caught their taxi-cab."

Braeden agreed. It would seem silly to have gates into heaven. Heaven isn't a physical place, at least not for angels, and that was all he could see. Braeden was wondering when he was going to start hearing God. Morgan had said that God has billions of conversations, but Braden hadn't heard any of them.

"That's because prayers are private," said Morgan.

"*Oh, I guess that makes sense,*" thought Braeden.

Morgan said, "If you can't see human souls, then why would you be able to hear their prayers to God? They can't communicate with you. Even if a human soul is dying in front of you and you are their Guardian, you can't assist until God gives the word. We take our orders from God, not humans. Remember that. Did you know that 'God' in whatever language, is the most commonly used word every single day on earth? Mortals today are so lazy that they don't even say it or text it, they just say O.M.G. for 'Oh my God', isn't that funny? We thought God would be upset but he's just happy that they are saying and thinking it, and bringing him into their world."

Braeden thought that was funny also. He replied back, "What does God say back to them when they say it or type it?"

Morgan laughed and said, "The same thing he always says, *'Yes, I am your God'*."

"What does he say when we say *'God love me'*?" asked Braeden.

Morgan gave him a really funny look, like he should know the answer.

"Come on, Braeden, I know you were only born twenty-five years ago, but you should know this one by now."

Braeden pondered for a moment before he said, "God says, 'I *am* loving you'."

Morgan flashed a huge grin and said, "Yes! He *can* be taught!"

They both laughed together. He really liked Morgan. He wasn't sure why, but he felt like he knew her already.

There sure was a lot to learn about being an angel. They floated down another great, long hallway until they came to a large, open area. There were five gigantic columns that formed a circle. He looked up and they went as high as he could see. At the very top, he could see blue sky and white clouds. He could see angels flying up through the clouds from all over.

"What's up there?" asked Braeden.

Morgan looked at him, and again gave him the same funny look. She said, "Come on, Braeden, you can do it. Think."

He replied, "Is that where God is?"

She giggled and said, "Well, God is everywhere, but he does actually have an office, and that is where it is. Actually, what you are witnessing is the A.C.C., Angel Command Center. Just above it is Father's office. You probably won't get to go in there for a little while. Usually it is just the Angel of the Lord, Angel of Light, and the Official Heralds that go into the office. Everyone is on A.B.L., Angel Bracelet Link." She pointed to her gold armband that was glowing.

To the left, Braeden could see a magnificent body of water that looked like an escalator. It was going up and down at the same time. He saw some very different non-human, angel-looking beings swimming up and down in the water. He turned to Morgan and asked her what they were.

She said, "We aren't the only ones up here. You can't see human souls, but you can see other things. Human souls are not the only creatures that get reborn. Wait until you go to Atlantis!"

It seemed like heaven went on forever. Aleona giggled and said, "Heaven *does* go on forever. You're right, Morgan, he's a funny one."

To the right he saw what looked like an airport walk-way made out of glass. It went as far as he could see, and there were clouds below it. He could see some angels walking across the walkway. Some of them were flying with their wings extended, and he could also see little balls of light zipping around.

"Come, this glass walkway is the way we need to go," said Taylor.

They all turned and kept walking down the beautiful, glass walkway. Braeden turned to Morgan and said, "We went to see the birth of baby Jesus. It was amazing. I saw you there, but you were busy."

Morgan smiled and said, "Yes, I saw you there too. Although it appeared to be a memory, it lives in the library, which means I am connected to it and all of its experiences at all times, so even when it appears I am not there, I am. The next time that you experience an event in the library, and I am there, I will be sure to let you know that I am also aware of you."

Braeden grabbed onto Morgan's hand and said, "Thanks, I would like that."

Taylor grabbed Aleona's hand and the four of them all said, "God love me." Braeden didn't know where they were going, but that was okay, as he knew that the rest of them did.

Taylor thought to him, *"We are going to twinkle the rest of the way. It's a lot faster. We are going to see Enyah, the Angel of Music. She resides here in heaven, with God and human souls, and oversees all the muses. You can decide if you want to be an Angel of Music."*

Braeden thought that was a really cool idea. He loved music and hoped he could play a harp or something. Throughout both Angel Academy and heaven he heard soft, melodious music. He thought, *"What does an Angel of Music do?"*

Aleona thought back, *"They make music, of course."*

There was a flash and an explosion of gold and silver glitter, and then the four of them twinkled to see the heavenly Angel of Music.

7

Angels of Music

There was a sparkle of gold glitter dust and a poof of smoke, and then the four little angels were in a different part of heaven. They had skipped the very long, glass walkway, which was fine by Braeden. He looked around and beautiful, green gardens, flowers, and roses surrounded him everywhere he could see. There were beautiful shrubs in the shapes of animals and the scent of fragrant roses, hydrangeas, and magnolias was everywhere. He could hear chirping birds and the sound of flowing water. It was a garden of paradise. It was never-ending as far as he could see, and there were turquoise blue skies and cotton balls of clouds. For the first time, there was a great, big, bright sun. It was amazing. If someone were to ask him what heaven looked like, for him, this would be it.

Toward the center, there was a floating waterfall exploding into fantastic water displays. Below, there was another circular, Roman column-type of area, with five giant, white columns. It was all outdoors, but looked somewhat like an indoor stage or a platform. They all walked toward it and saw a beautiful, young angel playing a golden harp. She was humming along to it. She smiled and looked up at her guests. She, like all of her fellow angels, wore a simple, silver-white tunic. She had dark, long hair that was braided in an intricate design, and she wore diamonds in her hair that sparkled in the sunlight. She had a gold bracelet on, but instead of sandals like Braeden and Taylor were wearing, she wore gold and black high-heels.

"Welcome to the garden of angels. My name is Bernice, and I am the Keeper of the Gardens. You are always welcome to come visit, and stay as long as you like. Many of the Muse Angels spend what seems like an eternity composing and creating here. There are human souls here, but they cannot see you. If you sing, however, they will hear the melody on Angel Radio."

Braeden walked over to Bernice and asked her, "Did you learn to play the harp when you became an angel? It's just absolutely beautiful."

Bernice smiled and said, "Yes, I am an Angel of Music. Human souls can hear my songs, and it inspires them."

Braeden asked, "If I became an Angel of Music, would I play a harp?"

Bernice said, "You can play whatever you want. When you talk with Enyah, you will know if you are meant to be an Angel of Music. But you should wait, and talk with all of the Senior Angels before you decide what you want to be. It took me five hundred years before I finally decided. So, don't hurry."

The little party of five made their way down past a tropical paradise of turquoise blue waters until they came to a small island about a mile from shore. Braeden looked over at Taylor. Taylor grabbed his hand and said, "I'll twinkle you over there."

Braeden wanted to twinkle on his own, but he still didn't know how. He didn't really mind that much, but he was anxious to learn. A poof of gold Angel Dust exploded around them and they found themselves on the island. Braeden looked over at Morgan and asked her, "Are we still in heaven?"

She smiled and said, "Yes, this is still heaven. It's just a slice of what it can be. Enyah does a lovely job of creating an inspiring place for composers, wouldn't you say?"

Braeden heard a melodious, "Thank you, you are *ever* so kind." The voice was like listening to chimes.

Enyah stood there, also in a silvery-white, glowing gown and a glowing halo. She wore a gold nametag that said "Senior Angel". She looked exotic, like she was a supermodel. She had long, black hair, and long, black eyelashes. Braeden almost forgot that everyone in heaven dressed really nicely, and suddenly he felt underdressed.

"Hello, Braeden, welcome to the Garden of Angels, and welcome to our little island," said Enyah.

The island began to transform into a decorated banquet hall with a total of five large, white columns separating different areas. There were white flowers decorating the hall, organized in impressive designs. It looked divine, and he wondered if this was all for him.

"Yes, little Braeden, this is your Coronation Ceremony, and this is your first stop in helping you determine what kind of angel you want to be. But you can't do that properly without any instruments. I'd like to present you with your first gift as an angel." She held out her hand and a small poof of smoke exploded. A small, gold bracelet appeared.

"This is an angel bracelet. It allows you to channel your Angel Dust to create musical instruments."

He walked over and said, "Thank you, Enyah, I am *ever* so grateful."

She replied, "Just think of a harp and it will appear."

He put the bracelet on and thought of a harp. POOF! With a small puff of smoke, a harp appeared. "Wow, that's so cool! So this is how Angel Dust works."

Braeden held out his left arm, admiring the gold bracelet. It sparkled in the sun. He knew that it could do more than just make harps and chimes. He could use it to make a weapon, like a sword or a shield.

Taylor interrupted his thinking, and said out loud, "Yes, this is the means by which an angel uses Angel Dust or Angel Energy. It is permanently bonded to your essence forever. The only way it can ever come off is if you disobey God. Then, you will lose your angel powers. It is also your means of communicatation with God and other angels. If you become a Guardian, you will also be able to hear human thoughts while in their presence. You would be able to hear humans, but they would not be able to hear you. Many Guardians don't last because they find it to be a lonely occupation, never being seen but always hearing."

Braeden had all kinds of questions and wondered what the best occupation was. He didn't want to get put into a job and then find out later that there was a better one. Now that he had a magic bracelet, he wasn't sure he wanted to be an Angel of Music. Being a Guardian sounded cool, but he hadn't met a Warrior Angel yet, and he didn't know what a Light Angel did. He was pretty sure that he wanted to hear from God more often, so maybe he could be a Herald or a Messenger. There were also angels who didn't even protect souls on earth, but were on different planets and dimensions altogether. The possibilities he learned about each day, each year, made it more difficult to choose. Plus, he really wanted to go talk with Marcia and meet the Cupids. He wondered when he was going to be able to go back to the library. There were all kinds of events in the past that he wanted to attend.

All of the sudden he heard a male voice that sounded like it was coming through a P.A. (public announcement) system. *"Hello, my little angels. There is trouble on earth and I need all squadron leaders to take their posts on full alert. Senior Angels, please report to my office."*

Braeden looked over at Taylor and wondered what was going on.

Taylor thought to him, *"Well, in case you hadn't guessed, that was Father. Enyah and all of the other Senior Angels are going to be busy, so it might not be the best time to go visit Marcia. How about going somewhere a lot different?"*

Braeden was sort of disappointed. He wanted to be in the private meeting with the other Senior Angels. Taylor broke his thoughts and said, "Why don't we go to another dimension? How about somewhere really cool! How about we go to ATLANTIS!"

Braeden grabbed Taylor's hand, and looked over at Morgan, Aleona, and Bernice. Braeden said, "Are you beautiful angels joining us?"

Morgan replied, "You have fun with Taylor. I will be joining you as soon as I report in to my squadron leader. I may be needed on earth."

With a flash and a twinkle, Morgan was gone. Aleona twinkled out too, and the two boys were left standing there with Bernice.

Bernice said, "Oh, I'm not a Senior Angel, and I never leave my beautiful garden of paradise. Thank you *ever* so much for the invitation."

Together, Braeden and Taylor said, "God love me," and then they were a poof of gold dust scattered on the floor.

8

History Lesson: Atlantis — Rise & Fall

Braeden was super-excited. He had always hoped that there was a place called Atlantis, but he had never thought in his wildest dreams that he would ever get to go there. Then again, as a human, he had never thought that he would be an angel. Since he hadn't even known that Atlantis existed, he wasn't sure where Atlantis was.

With a flash of gold light there was an explosion of angel glitter dust, and he and Taylor landed. "Jesus love me," they both said.

Braeden looked around at this new land. This was indeed something spectacular that he never could have even imagined. For years he thought it was just a lost city underwater, hidden deep below the sea somewhere on earth... someplace that neither man nor machine could get to. He looked at Taylor and wondered why he wasn't in God's office with the rest of the Senior Angels.

Taylor thought to him, "*The library is one of the few areas that is exempt from attacks on earth.*"

Braeden turned to Taylor and noticed that they were not alone. Another tall, blond angel was standing next to them. He was young, handsome, and muscular, and was also wearing an identical silver tunic. He had very large, extended wings, and his wings and halo were glowing. He appeared to be young, like a teenager's age on earth, but Braeden knew better. He was carrying a long, golden staff with a large, winged ball on the top. He spoke in a very deep, baritone voice and said, "Hello, Taylor, and welcome to Atlantis, Braeden. My name is Cameron. I am the official Herald for Atlantis, and while the Senior Angel is in a meeting with Father, I am here to assist you." His wings collapsed onto the floor, littering it with a little pile of Angel Dust. Braeden thought that he looked a lot like a lifeguard with his tan complexion. He felt like Cameron should be wearing sunglasses.

Cameron said, "Thanks, I'll take that as a compliment."

Braeden had forgotten that everyone could hear his thoughts. He gazed around at the magnificent city. It wasn't underwater, it wasn't even on earth. He looked up and he could see the night sky, three moons, and up in the distant left, a nebula. It was absolutely breathtaking. To the right he could see three suns, all burning different colors. Two suns rotated around the larger sun. One sun was green, the other was blue, and the largest one was pink and purple. They did not look anything like what the stars in the sky looked like from earth, or from Angel Academy.

The legends were true, Atlantis was beneath the deep blue seas. He had no idea how far or deep the water went up, and it was very different looking up into the water, instead of down. Up in the distance, directly above him, he could see what looked like an enormous, crystal blue body of water, like a lake floating in mid-air. There were water species that he had never seen before, and they were dancing in the water in front of him. They definitely were not fish. Five little water fairies swam by, pointing and waving to him. Braeden smiled and waved back.

An elegant, graceful, blue-winged creature gently fluttered toward him. As it got closer it transformed into a blue-skinned fairy. She looked like a miniature butterfly with long, floating blue hair, flowers for antennas, and to Braeden's surprise, not one, but two sets of wings. He shouldn't be *that* surprised, he was an angel after all... why *wouldn't* he see things like blue-skinned fairies?

Braeden turned to Cameron and said, "Can you please tell me where in the universe Atlantis is located? Since we twinkled here, I don't really know where we are. Or is it a secret? Maybe I'd like to be an Atlantean Angel."

Cameron flashed a big grin, showing his pearly white teeth. "Of course, I'll tell you. It's not a secret to you anymore now that you are an angel." He waved his large staff above them and a duplicate of earth and its surrounding planets shone above them. "This is Earth," he pointed.

What seemed to be a very long way away on the

model was a tiny planet, with three moons and three suns burning different colors.

"Here is Atlantis. If you were to try to get here you would have to go through three black holes and a supernova. It's pretty safe here."

Well, that just about summed up why they twinkled there. He certainly didn't want to go through three black holes and a supernova. He didn't know if angels could catch on fire, but he didn't want to find out. Taylor and Cameron started laughing.

Taylor said, "No, you can't catch on fire from a supernova. You *can* catch on fire from an Angel Light Arrow if you are a demon, although you would be up against an Angel of Light, and I'd have to say your chances of survival would be slim."

They walked down an ornate, large hallway, very similar to Angel Academy in that there were gigantic columns that went miles up into the sky. Also like heaven and Angel Academy, there were clouds at the top.

"Cameron, are there human souls here?" asked Braeden. He wasn't sure if this was just another copycat version of Angel Academy.

Cameron chuckled and said, "Oh, no. There haven't been human souls here for a very long time. Atlantis is now home to some of God's other amazing creations. The Senior Angel, Desiree, oversees this area. All of the mythical creatures are safe here. It is pretty spectacular."

For the first time, Braeden thought that he could manifest wings and fly. He kept concentrating, turning and looking at his back, but nothing happened. Taylor and Cameron started laughing.

Cameron said, "One thing at a time. You have to earn your wings and halo. For now, all you can do is create small objects, like musical instruments and such. When you meet the Senior Angel of the Warriors you will learn how to forge your sword, and when you meet the Senior Angel of the Cupids you will carry your first bow."

Braeden felt a little silly trying to make wings when he couldn't. He was appreciative that Cameron was nice enough to tell him these things. Now he really had something to look forward to when meeting the other Senior Angels. But what Braeden didn't realize was that he didn't actually need wings to fly. Now that he had a gold bracelet, he could float and fly short distances without having wings. He already knew how to turn into a ball of light.

Taylor said, "Wings are just for show. All angels can fly once they have their Angel Bracelet. Angels can be a little showy sometimes. You'll get used to it."

They walked a little further until they came to a very long, circular staircase that wrapped around a very large, circular opening below. Braeden could see stairs that would take a very long time to walk down. He looked over at Taylor and watched as he and Cameron slowly jumped, and floated down to the bottom which seemed like it was a mile down. Cameron was kind of a showoff and extended his wings, lighting up his halo. Heralds were always used to making a big entrance.

Cameron locked over at Braeden as he floated down, and said, "If you become a Herald you will learn that it is procedure to always extend your wings and light up your halo when descending from the skies. It also helps you to see where you are landing."

When he finally touched down, he was again amazed at what he saw. All around him were creatures that he had never seen before, suspended in water that, again, he had to look up in the air to see. This time, fairies weren't what caught his eye, instead it was a beautiful woman with a fish tail.

9

Queen Andromeda

For a moment, Braeden thought he was in a dream. He'd thought that Mermaids were made up, make believe... only in stories. He'd had no idea that they really existed. He actually remembered a television special that featured mermaids and it had turned out the whole thing was a hoax. The only reference that he had to mermaids was his copy of Disney's *The Little Mermaid,* and he was pretty sure that this was nothing like the cartoon he saw so many years ago. Taylor and Cameron weren't phased at all by the mysterious, beautiful maiden who was floating in front of them. He smiled at the pretty, young mermaid and finally said, "Hello, my name is Braeden. I am extremely honored to meet you, my lady."

She swam several large circles in the giant, overhead waters and smiled back. He noticed that several little angel goldfish were swimming in sync with her. It was very hypnotic.

She thought back to him, "*Greetings, Braeden. Welcome to Atlantis. My name is Andromeda. I am the Queen of the Mermaids and the Ruler of Atlantis.*" She looked over at Cameron and hissed, "You are dismissed."

Cameron glared at Andromeda, and his wings exploded in gold dust as he shot up to the top of the staircase. There appeared to be some sort of history between the two of them.

She, like the blue fairy, had long, blue hair that had streaks of black and white in it. Her skin had a blue tint to it and her mermaid tail was exotic, like those of the angel goldfish. Like her hair, her fins floated around her everywhere. Her tail was an iridescent color that changed from blue to purple.

Braeden thought that angels ruled Atlantis, but evidently there were some things that he didn't know.

Two other mermaids and two mermen, male merpeople, were floating above Andromeda about three hundred feet high in the water. Braeden hadn't noticed them at first. The mermaids were beautiful but the mermen were scary-looking. Braeden thought for sure that they must be Andromeda's personal guards, as they all carried trident-like pitchforks. Their tails were not shaped like angel fish tails, instead they were shaped like shark tails.

These mermen, while very muscular in appearance, wore black masks that covered their black eyes. They were also five times the size of the beautiful mermaids. They bore different tattoo-like designs across their entire bodies, and when they turned in the water overhead, the shark-like fins on their backs could be seen. However, unlike a shark's fin, theirs also had what appeared to be a large blade extending from the top; a deadly weapon, easily capable of slicing into a predator from below. Their tails also had blades on each side, and on top, forming a three-sided weapon. Each of their arms bore another knife-like fin, extending from wrist to elbow. Also unlike sharks, the length of their tails were very long, extending more than ten meters, and looked like they could be used to crush something as big as an anaconda snake. These guards looked fierce and were built to kill or protect. Anyone who messed with them would be foolish to think they were going to win.

Andromeda, now floating with four attendants next to her, looked even more intimidating and frightening. She thought to Braeden, *"Angels oversee this land. I, however, am the Queen, and for over seven thousand years, merpeople have occupied and inhabited Atlantis. Angels are welcome anytime. Come, I will share with you the story of Atlantis."*

The magic waterways floated around each of the merpeople so they were always encapsulated in water. It was almost like they were flying. Andromeda started swimming down into an underwater escalator like the one that Braeden had seen in heaven. It was at that point when he realized that it *had* been a mermaid he had seen in heaven. Braeden and Taylor floated over to the escalator, and Braeden wondered how he was going to go down it.

Taylor knew was he was thinking and said, "Angels can't burn, drown, or suffocate. We just float along; you can even go into the water if you want. Those mermen can't hurt you either. They look scary but they are the Queen's personal bodyguards. There are thousands more just like them that keep order and peace throughout Atlantis."

Braeden thought that was a good thing. He didn't think he would die as an angel anytime soon. He was curious about what *other* powers he had or what else he was capable of doing.

Taylor smiled and said, "Soon, my friend. Only another two hundred years to go and you'll be spreading your wings and flying on your own. Have you thought about what it is you want to do?"

Braeden floated alongside him for a few minutes before he finally said, "I'm sorry, Taylor. I don't know yet. Being in Atlantis is really amazing, but so is being in the Garden of the Angels. Can I decide after I get my bow?"

Taylor smiled back and said, "Of course you can. I was just wondering if there was something that had caught your eye."

Braeden was anxious to hear about Atlantis. For starters, how did it get here, where was it before, and why did it fall? What happened to it when it fell, and how did the merpeople get it? He followed the five merpeople and the angel fish down the long escalator of water. When they arrived at the bottom there was a beautiful, ornate chamber that looked like the inside of a gigantic oyster. Like the few places Braeden had witnessed in heaven and Angel Academy, it was encompassed by large, white columns on each side of the room. In the middle was a large chair where Andromeda had positioned herself. The two shark bodyguards floated next to her, and the two mermaids sat on coral reef chairs on each side. There was no sun, but bright lights shone through the top of the room as if there had been. Beautiful, fish-like creatures swam all over the room. Watching all of the water creatures was a show in itself.

"Please be seated," said the Queen.

The room was alive with so many interesting creatures. The floor started to shift and two chairs that looked like large pearls appeared for Taylor and Braeden to sit on. They sat down and were surprised at how comfortable they actually were. The chairs started to lean back, and again they were looking up at the ceiling. The room shifted once more and the lights overhead began to dim, almost as if they were in a theater.

The mermaid to Andromeda's left, Lindsey, had really long, pink hair, and a matching pink tail that changed colors. The mermaid positioned on Andromeda's right had a glowing light that softly shone on her, almost like a spotlight. She had really long, purple hair and wore black pearls around her neck. Like the Queen, her tail matched her hair. It was almost iridescent and change colors continuously. She was extremely beautiful. Braeden wondered if she was one of those mermaids that lured sailors to their deaths. She looked like she was wearing purple eye shadow and lipstick. "Welcome to the Throne Room. My name is Shayla, and I am the Queen's Chancellor, second in command for Atlantis. Behold, as I show you the story of our destruction and creation."

The lights dimmed above them and what appeared was an exact image of the great city of Atlantis while it had still been on earth and inhabited by human mortals. The city became larger until Braeden could actually see people within it.

Shayla started saying, "Humans fought for centuries above our home, thousands of miles above the waters. We, as merpeople, never had any reason to fear these humans, and we ignored them for centuries until, one day, they destroyed themselves in a great war that lasted for a thousand years. The city changed and was attacked by flying aircraft, shot at by great battleships in the sea, and by large spaceships in the air. Finally, there was an explosion so bright you had to cover your eyes. Those who had not escaped in lifepods were instantly vaporized."

What happened next was so remarkable that Braeden thought he was in the library back in Angel Academy. Hundreds of thousands of angels twinkled in all over the city, each of them taking souls in each hand and twinkling out just as fast as they came in. It was like watching a firework show. This went on for only a few minutes, and then the magnificent city began to sink. Water from all sides began to flood the city walls. The protective barrier shield had been destroyed during the human war, and the weight of the water forced the city underwater.

"The City of Mermaids was a peaceful place. Deep beneath the sea, where the pressure was too great for any man or machine, lived millions of mermaids and mermen. The merpeople only had moments before their home would be crushed by Atlantis," continued Shayla.

Braeden sat watching, terrified for the merpeople. He could see innocent little children who would die. He shouted out, "Noooo!!"

Queen Andromeda smiled. She liked that this new angel felt pity and compassion for her people.

Shayla continued the story, narrating, "The City of Mermaids was a magical place. It, too, was protected by magic, but nothing could stop it from being crushed by something so large and so heavy. Hundreds of the Chimera, enormous, winged, underwater creatures, came out of the dark shadows to try to protect the city from destruction. Despite them being a thousand times larger than humans, they were not strong enough to lift or move a city. It would only be moments until millions of lives were lost."

An image of the Queen flashed in front of them. She was in a praying position with her hands close to her heart. "My people," she said, "destruction is upon us. There is no time to evacuate. Please, pray to God for help."

The scene shifted and millions of merpeople could be seen stopping to pray to God. Then the scene changed once more and Atlantis was no longer in view. Instead, it was clearly the Angel Command Center in Angel Academy. A new angel that Braeden had never seen before sat at the helm of a very busy office, and was shouting out orders and instructions to different areas of the command center. It was Senior Angel, Aaron, giving commands to the other operators. Since Braeden hadn't actually been in the A.C.C. yet, this was all very exciting for him.

Aaron was different from any of the other angels he had seen. Aaron was an Asian angel. He, too, was beautiful, and he looked exotic. He wore a similar silver tunic, a gold headset on his right ear, and a matching gold nametag that read "Aaron, Senior Angel, A.C.C.". He definitely looked like a leader or like someone in charge.

Another angel, Ia, was floating around down lower in the command center, giving orders and supervising other angels. She wore a gold headset over her head that had a microphone floating in front of her right cheek. She would occasionally touch it, look at Aaron, say something, and then respond back. There were six other angels who had on similar headsets.

Ia flew up two levels and shouted, "HALT! EMERGENCY, PRIORITY GOLD!"

All of the angels stopped what they were doing and looked at Aaron. The room was silent and still for what seemed like forever, but in fact was really only a minute. Aaron twinkled out of the command center and, just as fast, twinkled back. His halo and wings were shining gold. He radiated brightly, causing the other angels to activate their sunshades to cover their eyes.

Aaron touched his headset, and said loud and clear so that it could be heard all throughout heaven and Angel Academy, "God has spoken. All angels are on priority alert. We are saving all of the merpeople and the city of Atlantis. Activate the Delta Sequence."

In a flash, all of the angels everywhere, in all realms and dimensions, twinkled to Atlantis and the City of Mermaids. They surrounded the city in a glorious ball from all sides. With their gigantic, gold wings extended, it was a magnificent sight. At the same time, every angel in the universe said, "God love me," and then both cities twinkled as one, great big twinkle. In a flash of light, the City of Atlantis would be lost to humanity forever and the secret City of Mermaids would never be known to man.

All the while, Braeden and Taylor sat there staring at the ceiling. As Braeden watched, he thought that he had a pretty good idea of where it went from that point. He thought that the show was over, but he was mistaken. The lights shined back onto Shayla, and she continued with her tale.

"Atlantis was enormous, once home to over a million humans. The City of Mermaids had been twinkled inside of the very center of Atlantis, which could easily hold a city ten times the size of the City of Mermaids."

Millions of angels floated around, surrounding the city. Seeing so many angels like this was amazing. They were awaiting instruction. Across the skies the angels' bracelets could be seen as they lit up and glowed. A very familiar voice announced, "*Thank you, my darling angels. Merpeople, your prayers were heard and answered. Welcome to your new home, located far away from earth.*"

In response, he heard millions of merpeople praying back, "Thank you, God."

Then, in a flash, the millions of angels all twinkled, leaving the city covered in Angel Dust.

The light focused back on Shayla. "Since that time we have lived peacefully in this magical realm created just for us. Do you have any questions?" she asked.

Of course, Braeden had questions. He always had

questions. He raised his hand like he was in a classroom.

Shayla smiled and said, "Yes, little angel Braeden, what would you like to know?"

Braeden liked her. He put his hand down and said, "When did all the magical creatures get put here?"

She looked at Taylor instead of responding, and he acknowledged her by answering, "When Aaron activated the Delta sequence it did more than just twinkle an entire civilization and their home to another dimension. It activated angels from *all* realms and dimensions, and it took all the mythical creatures for protection. God said that he never wanted his creatures to be in harm's way as a result of human impact. So when that happened, fairies, unicorns, and even some big 'baddies' that you never want to run into, were all twinkled here to this small, paradise planet."

Braeden said, "Can merpeople or any other creature leave Atlantis and go back to earth?"

No one said anything and the room was silent. Finally Queen Andromeda answered, "Why would they ever want to leave? Merpeople and its inhabitants do not have the power of teleportation. It requires a holy relic from an angel, Angel Dust, or a twinkle to get in or out of Atlantis."

Taylor then added, "There are mercenary angels who will twinkle for a price. We don't really talk about them very much. They're not really angels you want to be associated with due to their... tactics and prices."

Braeden wasn't exactly sure what the tactics and prices included, but he was pretty sure that if you were "dealing" with an angel who went rogue, it couldn't be good. There was more that he wanted to know but he felt he had asked enough questions for now.

Braeden did not realize it but they had spent a really long time in Atlantis. In fact, they had spent so much time that Morgan came looking for them. When they got to the top of the water escalator she was standing there. She no longer had on her silver gown, but instead was wearing battle gear armor; she had on a battle helmet and carried a long silver sword. In place of her high-heeled shoes were heavy boots that looked like they were used for kicking. She looked fierce and terrifying.

"Come," she said, "your training is going to be cut short. There is a war brewing."

10

The Kaiatu - Fallen Angels

"A war is brewing?" asked Braeden. "With who?" He wanted to know.

"With whom?" she replied back. "The same ones who are always at war. The humans. They are always fighting over something."

Morgan was like a totally different angel. Whatever had happened while he was in Atlantis was not going over well with her. He leaned over and kind of nudged her with his shoulder. She looked at him, still with no emotion in her eyes or face.

"Hey, Morgan. What's wrong, other than the war brewing? You don't seem like yourself." He blinked twice hoping for some kind of response.

"Braeden, you don't understand because you are so new. There is something very terrible brewing, and Warrior Angels all over earth are standing by for whatever is going to happen."

He was about to ask if she knew what was going to happen when she looked over at him and said, "Only God and the prophet, Jocelyn, who made this claim, know what is going to happen, *if* it happens. This is not the first time we have been put on alert only to find out nothing has happened."

He walked a few steps and then finally said, "It's not the end of the world, is it?" He was hoping he would get to see the world as an angel before it all ended.

She stopped and took off her helmet. She held it in her right hand, while she gripped her sword with her left. She said, "No, it's not the end of the world. But it is possible that millions of lives will be lost for a stupid reason. Do you know how much work it will cause heaven and all the angels if this happens? We are in no way prepared to start taking in this many souls." She shook her head and kept walking.

Taylor was walking alongside him and whispered into his ear, "Morgan likes to get all gussied up in battle gear, but it's very unlikely that she is actually going to fight anyone, unless this really doesn't have anything to do with humans and is another battle for their souls instead." He rolled his eyes and spoke really loudly, "Morgan! Have the Kaiatu been scaring you again?"

This was obviously a sensitive subject for her. She turned with a glare, didn't say anything, and kept on walking.

Braeden asked, "What is the Kaiatu and what just happened here?"

Taylor grinned like he was in on a dirty secret. He reached over and touched his gold bracelet to Braeden's. Then something amazing happened... Taylor was able to *think* to Braeden, and no angel or other creature could hear them. Only God himself could hear what they were thinking.

"This activates a really cool feature that Sasha, Senior Angel of Angel Technology, developed a few thousand years ago when the Kaiatu were formed. It allows angels to have private conversations. You haven't noticed yet, but

there are all kinds of chatter going on and it can be a little busy sometimes.

"The Kaiatu are a band of misfits. And when I say misfit, I mean that they never should have been angels or even been close to heaven. They are what humans would call 'fallen angels'. We don't ever talk about them, as acknowledging them just gives them power. Morgan's had a few run-ins with the Kaiatu, and as a result she wants to strike and attack them."

Taylor continued with his story: "A long time ago there was an angel crime that took place. A Kaiatu slayed a Cupid and stole its red ruby heart. The Angel Bracelet was also stolen, and that was the first time, ever, that evil had had two holy relics as weapons. A demon is not powerful enough to kill a Cupid, but another angel is. That red ruby has immeasurable power, and it fell into the hands of a human mortal named Diana. She ate the heart and became immortal. The Romans treated her like a Goddess and worshiped her. Without Angel Dust to power it, the bracelet was eventually rendered useless. After years of searching for it, it appeared to be lost forever."

Braeden was getting anxious again. He was learning more things than he had ever learned as a mortal. So, obviously it was true that an angel could fall from heaven and... then what? Did an angel become a demon if they fell? And what was so upsetting to Morgan? Was he ever going to find out? He was sure that if he could just go to the library he could find out everything that happened back then, including stuff that was written in the Bible. Was that allowed? Couldn't Taylor just tell him?

Braeden thought, "*If an angel falls, do they lose their powers? Can you tell me what happens so I don't accidentally do it? I'd really like a lesson in some rules.*"

Taylor nodded and agreed. He touched his bracelet to Braeden's again, and the secure link was broken. Taylor said, "That's a really good idea, and while we are thinking about it, now would be a good time to visit Suzanne in Internal Affairs. She works in heaven in the Angel Command Center. She actually reports to Jefferson, who oversees the Angel Council. You will just love her. You know, it's not an accident that you automatically love an angel but fear a demon. An angel is full of God's love. A demon has no love of God in it, but instead is filled with hate."

Braeden knew what "Internal Affairs" meant on earth. He had seen enough television shows about cops to know that they were the police for the police. Although, the word 'library' had a very different meaning here than it did on earth, so he wasn't sure what to expect from Internal Affairs in heaven. Everything was so new and different.

He looked at Taylor and said, "Shouldn't we be going where Morgan went? She made it sound like it was kind of important."

Taylor replied, "There will always be fighting, there will always be disagreement, and there will always be human mortals that will finish their time as mortals on earth. If I put on battle gear every time there was a fight, it would be insane. Morgan has fought in a lot of wars. She has slayed many demons, and, too many fallen angels. Come on, let's twinkle out of here and be in a more divine heavenly place... like heaven. Centuries of hearing about the end of the world tend to leave me a little insensitive."

Braeden definitely liked that idea. As much as he liked being in this cool, new, fantasy world, he didn't really care for the shark men. He knew that there was a story there... in fact, he knew that there were some amazing tales he would one day discover. He wondered how much angels interfaced with Atlantis, and what other incredible creatures there were. As a small planet, there were all kinds of God's magical mysteries hiding, just waiting to be discovered.

11

Morgan was a Guardian?

"When God talks, you listen," said Taylor.

It seemed like a pretty simple and obvious rule, thought Braeden. There were, however, many angels who had broken that rule.

Morgan interrupted and said, "What is the number one Angel Law that all angels *must* obey?"

Braeden looked at her kind of funnily and said, "What, is this a pop quiz or something?"

Morgan was not amused with his humor and threw down her helmet. "I'm serious, my little padawan.

Lest thee not forget that thee is an apprentice to me!"

He stepped back and said, "All angels must obey God. That is rule number one."

She relaxed and retracted her wings. She said, "I was afraid that thee had quickly forgotten who is whom." Braeden liked it when she used the word "thee" for "you".

Braeden was hoping that they would leave Atlantis soon. He really didn't like the feeling he was having right now. Taylor reached out his hand, and Braeden happily took it in his. They looked at each other and said, "God love me." This time when they said it, something different happened.

Braeden heard the same voice on the P.A. reply back, "I am *always loving you*," and he felt that same warm feeling in his heart again.

Braeden really liked this feeling and he was really excited to hear God in his head. Taylor squeezed his hand and they both said, "Jesus love me." Braeden hoped he would hear something back like he did when he said, "God love me," but instead there was silence.

In a flash and a cloud of gold dust, they were standing in heaven, looking up again at the Angel Command Center. All of the feelings of negativity that Braeden had had a few moments ago were gone. He looked up, and then over at Taylor. Before he could ask the question, Taylor said, "When you meet God for real, he will activate your Angel Bracelet and then you will hear him. It's all part of your Angel Orientation process. One thing at a time so you are not so overwhelmed."

"It's about time you guys finally got here," said a very familiar, female voice. It was Morgan, but this time she was her normal, sweet, angelic self. Whatever was going on in Atlantis wasn't going on here. Morgan was no longer in battle armor and instead had on another elegant, formal, white and silver evening gown. Her hair was pulled up in another up-do style. He noticed that this time she had little, sparkling diamonds in her hair. He couldn't see her feet, but he was pretty sure there were some gold and black high-heeled shoes under there. He was a little confused as to the sudden change in her appearance and attitude.

Morgan knew what he was thinking and said in her innocent angel voice, "Sorry to disappoint, but when you're in heaven, there is no way you can be mad at anything or anyone, especially when you look as ravishing as I do right now. God designed it so that there is no negativity in heaven."

Braeden had to admit that, once again, she looked dressed to impress.

She looked at Braeden and Taylor and said, "Don't you boys think it's about time that you cleaned up a little bit before you go in? I know that Father designed the little tunics, and they are cute and all, but come on!"

Braeden wasn't sure what he should do, so Morgan snapped her fingers and a cloud of gold dust swirled around him. Suddenly, he was no longer dressed in a tunic, but instead had on a fabulous, white Dolce and Gabana tuxedo, with gold cuff links shaped like coins, a white bow tie, and a pair of white Johnston Murphy patent leather shoes to match. His hair was cleaned up and he looked handsome.

Morgan said, " Love the shoes. Wingtips?"

Taylor grunted, "Mmmph," and snapped his fingers. A cloud of gold and silver dust exploded around him, and when the Angel Dust settled he was in a glowing, white Christian Dior tuxedo, almost identical to Braeden's. He also had gold cuff links, but his had an ornate, winged insignia instead of coins like Braeden's. His shoes were almost the same as Braeden's, and he was wearing his matching gold nametag on the right-hand side of his blazer. His bowtie was white with gold accents on each side, giving his nametag and bowtie an extra sparkle. His hair was also nicely styled, and he looked like he was going to the most formal event ever. His tuxedo was slightly different as he had tails on his jacket. He, too, looked amazing.

Braeden looked around and said, "Where's Aleona? Isn't she going to come with us?"

Morgan replied back, in an amazing rendition of an English accent, "I'm not her sitter, but last I heard, Caden said she was enroute to somewhere in England...a royal baby is about to be born or something. There is a quite a hoopla, and a ton of English folks have been praying for this baby."

Braeden said, "Who's Caden?"

Morgan replied back, still in her English accent, "Caden works for the Royal Sentry Guard that protects and oversees any soul on earth that is deemed 'royalty'. His office is located in the A.C.C."

In her normal voice, she said, "Don't act like he is a big deal or it will go to his already-big head. He also oversees 'celebrities', so he thinks he's holier than thou. But you may like him, who knows. And the answer is *no*, you can't choose Royal Sentry Guard as your occupation."

Taylor grinned and said in his best English accent, "Oh, my! Do I detect a slight hint of jealousy that someone was not selected to go along? If I am not mistaken it was *you* who was the official Herald for Princess Diana, and wasn't it a certain King Louis the something as well? Oh, and lest we not forget the official announcement and coronation of Prince Henry?"

Morgan responded back with an angelic, innocent smile, gracefully showing a smaller version of her wings and a glowing halo. She really did look like an angel.

Taylor laughed and said, "Okay, someone's just an innocent angel who never reminds anyone of her deeds that go unrewarded."

She laughed back and said, "*One* time I mention it, and I'll never hear the end of it."

The three of them walked a little bit through heaven. It seemed that everywhere they went in heaven it was very large, very impressive, and if you had to walk through it, it would take a month to get somewhere.

Fortunately, they didn't seem to walk for long before they were floating up toward the extremely large Angel Command Center. It seemed like everything in the universe was housed inside of it. Thousands of angels worked there, and it contained so many departments that Morgan was afraid Braeden would end up working there. There was always so much room for movement and promotion in the A.C.C., unlike being locked into being a Guardian for five human-lifetimes, which is the standard contract to be a Guardian. Morgan had always felt that being a Guardian was harder than anything else she'd had to do, and she had been in *so* many roles as an angel.

She had been a Guardian once upon a time, in a land far away. She had watched over a little boy named Nathan. Unlike in Angel Academy, time flowed differently on earth. Each day, she sat with Nathan and listened as his mother read him stories. His father would take him on walks, and Morgan would float alongside them as Nathan would run and play with his dog, Delilah, a cute little black and tan Miniature Pincher.

Although Nathan could never hear her, Morgan actually found this comforting and as a relief. She would sit and talk to Nathan about the hard times of being an angel, like about the things she had to do that she didn't want to but did anyway. Nathan would sometimes stop playing and act like he could hear her. Of course, that was impossible. Morgan had never had any children, but she could easily see why a former parent would want to be a Guardian. It was very much like raising a child.

One day, when Nathan was about five years old, he had been playing with Delilah, running along a stream. Delilah was an overzealous little dog and she could run really fast. Nathan couldn't hold the leash for very long and Delilah got loose. Morgan could actually *see* what was going to happen, and for the first time in Nathan's existence Morgan was there to do her job; guard and protect this little soul. In Morgan's mind, she saw a future vision of Delilah running close to the water, chasing after a squirrel. Nathan desperately ran after her, trying to catch up.

Delilah was running too fast and Nathan slipped and fell into the water, hit his head, and drowned. In her vision she saw Nathan die, and she got fired for letting a child's soul die, one of the worst crimes for a Guardian.

When Morgan's vision of the future ended, she had snapped back to the present and saw Nathan and Delilah heading toward the creek. With only moments to spare, she had to do something, anything, to save this child who was like a son to her. In her mind she could see the squirrel running toward them. She could also see Skye, an Angel of Death, floating overhead. Skye looked at Morgan and smiled. Skye pointed to Nathan and mouthed to her, "He's mine." Morgan knew that what she saw was no accident. If Skye was floating around, literally, then there was going to be a fight.

What happened next was so remarkable, time literally stopped for Nathan and Delilah. Morgan twinkled and was on another dimensional plane with Skye. She could still see earth, Nathan, the stream, and also the deadly squirrel that Skye had taken the form of.

"GET AWAY FROM HIM!" screamed Morgan. "HE IS AN INNOCENT CHILD!"

Skye laughed at her and shouted back, "You think this is *easy* and *fun* for me?"

Skye was beautiful and scary. In this other plane of existence, it was going to be an all-out battle for Nathan's soul. Skye's wings exploded in a cloud of black dust, showing black wings with giant feathers. She didn't have a halo but she was armed with a black sword and wore a black and silver shield on her left arm.

Morgan exploded in a cloud of gold dust, dressed in her battle armor. She had on large wing guards, protecting her giant wings. She, too, had a sword, but her sword was white and was on fire. White fire. She didn't have a shield, but she was carrying a gold bow over her shoulder.

Their swords clashed for the first time, and when they did, explosive thunder rumbled through the skies. The clear, blue skies were now covered in dark clouds. Morgan spun around, striking Skye's shield, and bounced off harmlessly.

Skye laughed and shouted back, "You are going to have to do much better than that, sister, if you are going to win this battle."

Morgan flew back a hundred feet, flying in loops and circles and attacking Skye from all sides.

What seemed like an eternity to Morgan lasted only seconds for Nathan. Morgan spun around while Skye was laughing, and hit her on the back with her sword. Lightening struck down in Nathan's world. Skye screamed out in response. Morgan was going to safeguard the "asset" at all costs. She was not going to get fired.

She flew up in the air in the astral plane, and drew her bow. She cried out loud, "God give me the strength to save this little boy!" Her A.B.L. lit up, and her friend, Edwin, a champion Cupid she had known for thousands of years, came online. A cloud of gold smoke appeared, and his handsome face was there.

He looked over at Skye, and then down at Nathan, and said, "Holy Toledo!" Then he disappeared, leaving Angel Dust behind.

At the exact same moment in time, Nathan's mother started looking around for her little boy. In a cloud of dust, Edwin appeared out of nowhere. Although Nathan's mother couldn't see Edwin, somehow she was able to hear him.

"Lucille! Nathan is in deep trouble and is about to die! Please, pray to God for help!"

Lucille thought that Nathan had been gone for what seemed like far too long. A mother just has those feelings, those intuitive feelings when something is wrong. She stopped, and for just a moment she prayed, and then said out loud, "God, please help me find my little boy!"

Back in the Angel Command Center, one of the angel operators flew up out of her station, yelling, "Halt! PRIORITY WHITE!"

The angel operator looked up at the Senior Angel, but he was not at his station. Instead, Xi, another beautiful, Asian-looking angel, stood in charge with a gold headset on. Xi looked at her, and in a flash she was gone. A second later, she twinkled back, glowing gold. She motioned at Ia, Section Leader, to take command, and Xi twinkled out of the A.C.C., instantly fighting next to Morgan.

Morgan looked over and said, "Hi, Xi, so glad to see you. As you can see, I am in a little bit of trouble. Thank the Lord you came to help. Nathan is about to slip and fall into the water. Skye has taken shape as that nasty squirrel."

Xi shouted out loud, "EDWIN!"

Then Edwin was not just a dust cloud image like before, but a full-fledged Guardian. Lucille's guardian, to be exact. The three of them had their weapons extended and they clashed, fought, and tore at Skye. They battled tirelessly against Skye, but she was very strong and managed to withstand their attacks.

Edwin thought to Lucille, "Come on, one more prayer," and then Lucille stopped and said, "Please, God!"

Then, Lucille heard Delilah barking outside in the distance. She ran out of the door screaming, "NATHAN! DELILAH!" She was answered by Delilah's little high-pitched bark, slowly drowning in the harsh wind from the dark storm clouds overhead.

Swords clashed in the dark skies, lighting them up with lightning. Instantly, a puff of gold dust exploded and there were five guardian angels all ready to do battle. It was eight to one, and at this point was not looking good for Skye. A black, see-through force shield surrounded her. All of the angels floated and flew around her, swords and bows extended. She screamed at them, "You are a bunch of cheating angels! Eight to *one*! This must be *some* child that you are protecting!"

She and the squirrel exploded in a cloud of black dust. Her departure was explosive as dozens of lightening bolts shot out, one of them hitting a tree next to Nathan, catching it on fire before it fell. Less than a meter away was his unconscious body, lying on the ground.

"Morgan? Hello, heaven to Morgan? Where are you?" said Braeden.

She snapped back to reality and out of the memory of her first asset. It was hard to protect and watch an asset while knowing that one day you would ultimately lose them.

Braeden was waving his hand in front of Morgan's face to get her attention. He was anxious to actually see inside of the A.C.C.. She wanted to warn Braeden that being a Guardian was hard, especially when you had to watch over the asset for their entire life. It was like raising a son or daughter, and then having to watch them die. Very hard.

She was going to keep Nathan a secret for now. Braeden needed to know what happens to bad angels. He needed to know about... the fallen. He needed to learn how angels are punished.

12

I Saw God

Thinking back to that day when she and Skye had fought for Nathan's life brought back more than one painful memory. She knew that she had almost lost the asset. The first time that she'd had to go to Internal Affairs was because of that day, and going back, even just for a visit with her newest angel, gave her the chills.

Morgan, Taylor, and Braeden were all standing in the great entryway into the A.C.C.. Once inside, it was even more grandiose than it appeared from the outside. It was gorgeous, and there were what appeared to be thousands of angels manning stations in front of computer screens that had no stands. All of this was floating in the air; little maps, charts, all kinds of things. It reminded Braeden of being in an airport control tower.

Taylor said, "That's exactly what this area is like. Controlling air traffic. In this case, the prayers are what are in the air instead of planes. Sometimes we control angels in the air, and sometimes we control the weather. Humans pray to us for good health and good weather the most. It's sort of strange, but if enough humans pray for sunshine and no clouds on a particular day, it goes through the same channels as a prayer for saving a life; it just doesn't have priority."

They walked a little further until they came to a reception area with a very large, circular desk. It was so tall that all three of them had to float up to it so they could see and talk to whoever was behind the counter.

A beautiful, young, dark-skinned, African American angel sat at the desk. She didn't have on a white tunic or a fancy ball gown. Instead, she wore a very sharp-looking business suit in all white. She had long hair that was pulled up in a very business-like style. She looked up and smiled. Her smile was beautiful and she had perfect, white teeth.

"Hello, Taylor and Morgan, welcome. And whom do we have here?" she said.

Taylor smiled back and said, "Hi, Imogene, it's nice to see you again. We're here to introduce Braeden to Suzanne. He's going to get a brief lesson on some rules. It's kind of funny seeing you up here at the front desk. Did you mouth off to Aaron again?" He laughed jokingly.

Imogene smiled politely back and touched her head-set with her right index finger. Imogene didn't say anything in response to his comment, but instead said, "Suzanne is finishing up a meeting. You can go ahead and walk down to her office. She should be done by the time you get there."

She pressed a button and the golden see-through gate that blocked their entry opened up. They went through it and started walking toward her office.

Morgan looked over at Taylor and said, "What was that all about?"

He chuckled and said, "Oh, a few thousand years ago Imogene thought that she should be a Senior Angel and went over Aaron's halo into God's office. Of course, he was forgiving, but there are rules in place for a reason, and you don't just go marching into God's office without permission. I was joking when I said, 'did she mouth off', but since Imogene didn't say anything and her thoughts were pure, we will never know unless she tells us."

Morgan then said, with the biggest smile, "*Or...* a Senior Angel over the library could just go into the angel archives and *find out* what happened."

Taylor gave Morgan a stern look. Braeden stopped walking and said, "You mean you can find out administration kinds of stuff in there? You could find out who I was before I was an angel?"

Morgan stopped and looked directly into Braeden's hazel eyes. For just a second she thought she saw something, and just as quickly it went away. It was just a glimpse, a glimmer of a vision, a window. There had been a look in his eyes that she knew too well.

Taylor looked at both of them and said, "Not in a million years will you ever use knowledge in such a manner. Shame on you for even thinking such a thing. And on you, Morgan, for letting Braeden even know that it is possible."

Braeden dragged his feet as he shuffled along the rest of the way. He sure had had a lot of disappointment in his first two hundred years of being an angel. As they approached Internal Affairs, Braeden saw two very large Warrior Angels with a smaller angel walking between them. They looked fierce, and the dark colors of their battle gear clashed with all of the white around them. The smaller angel had his hands tied together and they were bound with his halo. For the first time, he saw an angel lose his halo. His wings were still there but they looked like someone had beat them heavily and they were missing feathers. His left wing looked broken and it was dragging on the ground. It truly was a sad sight to see. All of the angels watched as he was escorted out of heaven.

Braeden heard a gasp, as if someone had seen a ghost. He turned, and Morgan and Taylor both had their mouths open, jaws almost to their chests. They both knew that particular angel, and the look on their faces showed that they were shocked. Braeden didn't know who the angel was, but he desperately wanted to, and to know what had happened to him. They didn't say anything but kept watching. It was Edwin.

Two extremely beautiful angels, Drake and Illana,

came out of Suzanne's office. One was a male and the other was female. Drake had blond hair and he was really tall. He wasn't dressed up for heaven, as he was half naked. He had very small wings that extended across his muscular back. He also had a muscular chest and "six-pack" abs. He didn't exactly have a tunic on, but a miniature version of one that was white, and had a tiny, little, sparkling ruby heart on it near the right side of his hip. He was wearing a gold bow over his shoulder, and there were a bunch of roses in his arrow case along with some white and silver arrows.

Illana had long, blond, almost white hair and the two of them looked like either the perfect couple or siblings. Illana wore her hair down, cascading down her back between her wings. She had on a very elegant, tight, form-fitting, white dress that stopped right before her shoes. Like Drake, her halo glowed brightly as she walked. She, too, had a ruby red heart, but it was not pinned onto her dress; instead it was suspended around her neck as a pendant. Like Drake, she was carrying arrows and roses on her back. She did not carry a bow, but in her left hand she wielded a gold crossbow. She wore white, high-heeled boots instead of gold sandals. She had a certain bounce in her step.

The two of them were laughing as they were talking and walking. Drake saw the three angels silently start walking over to them. Illana followed right behind. At the same time, they both looked at Braeden and said, "Hi there, handsome! Welcome to Angel Academy."

Drake said, "My name is Drake, and this is my cohort, Illana. If you hadn't guessed, we are Cupids and we would *love* for you to come join our ranks." They reached out their hands to shake Braeden's.

Morgan grabbed Braeden's hand and said, "Not so fast, you little love demons. You're not getting your love talons into him just yet. He can't even make a bow, so lay off." She stepped in between the two lovely Cupids and extended her wings.

Illana said, "My, someone is a little protective. Afraid you'll lose another apprentice to the Cupids?"

She and Drake both laughed, and then in a puff of gold dust and a flash of light they twinkled out of there.

Morgan retracted her wings and said, "Just a bunch

of showoffs. They don't have any real responsibilities, like saving lives."

She held onto Braeden's hand and started to lead him toward Suzanne's office, but stopped when she saw who was at the door. Next came Marcia, Senior Angel of Cupids and True Love, this time dressed very business-like in a white business suit with white high-heels, instead of gold. Braeden noticed her diamond bracelet and saw her ruby red heart dangling on her right wrist. She was talking with someone inside of the door that they couldn't see. She laughed, and then twinkled out in a cloud of dust.

Braeden asked, "Are all Cupids so..."

"Gorgeous?" said Morgan. "Unfortunately, yes. That little red ruby that you see clashing against our virgin-white outfits is what makes them so..." She didn't finish her sentence, almost like it pained her to. She was, instead, lost in a memory about Edwin and Nathan.

All three angels were staring at the door. When it opened, there stood Suzanne. She was talking to a gold ball of light the size of a basketball. She was laughing with it, and then it changed sizes, did a little light show, and shrank in size to be as small as an orb. It flew straight up through the A.C.C., past Senior Angel Aaron, and up into God's office.

Braeden had finally seen God.

13

Archangel

"Wow, this is so exciting. I finally saw God!" said Braeden.

His A.B.L. lit up and he heard a voice, the same on the P.A., say back, "*Yes, Braeden, and I saw you. Welcome to heaven. After you speak with Suzanne, I would love to see you in my office.*"

His past experiences being asked to be seen in someone's office had never been good. And never in his whole life did he ever think that he would get called into God's office. Just thinking about it got him excited. He hadn't done anything bad, so whatever it was, it could only be good.

Taylor looked at him and smiled. He thought, "*Yes, little angel. It is definitely something good, and something to really look forward to experiencing. Morgan and I cannot enter without permission, so you will go alone. You are so blessed.*"

"I didn't think I'd get to see God today," said Braeden.

He heard a new, chirpy, happy voice say, "Not get to see God in heaven? Well that would just ruin my whole day!"

Braeden looked over and saw a beautiful, female angel who appeared to be a little bit older than he and his cohorts, he couldn't really tell for sure. She had golden hair that was pulled up in an elegant hairdo. She had on stylish glasses that had a little gold chain on them, and she wore a business dress-suit that stopped at her knees. She had on black, high-heeled shoes with gold accents on them. The suit, unlike any other outfit he had seen on an angel, had black on it. She looked very sophisticated. She also wore a gold nametag. Hers, however, was engraved with a new title he had never seen before.

Suzanne, Archangel

Braeden had never met an Archangel and was a little taken back. Suzanne sensed what he was feeling and said, "No need to be afraid, sweetheart. For now, I'm your friend."

By her making that statement, Braeden felt like she had probably lost a lot of friends. She reached out and touched his hand. He felt a cool sensation he had never felt before. It felt good, and he liked it.

She said, "That is what *truth* feels like."

She let go of his hand and all of the sudden he was very willing to do whatever she asked of him... Braeden wasn't quite sure why, but Morgan knew. It was because an Internal Affairs Angel's touch is like truth serum. It makes anyone tell the absolute truth, with no way around it. Their touch also made subjects lethargic and more willing to go somewhere or follow someone. She motioned for the three of them to go into her office.

"I see you've met a couple of Cupids outside of my office. Nicely done, Morgan, thwarting that handshake."

Morgan smiled and said, "Yes, Suzanne, I have

encountered enough Cupids to know not to let any-one touch them."

Braeden looked over and thought, "*Why?*"

Suzanne said, "As you may have noticed, when you touch an angel you feel something... each one feels different. It is part of their gift, their powers. Cupids are designed to make people fall in love. People who fall in love will usually do just about anything, for anyone, when they are under a Cupid Trance. If you would have touched both of them, there would have been no chance for you to take any occupation other than a Cupid. And, as Morgan knows, that's not really fair, is it?"

Suzanne's office was enormous and looked like it could hold hundreds of angels. He glanced around and realized that it was set up very much like a court-room, with a place for witnesses, a jury, and lots of seating. There was a very large, glass, boardroom-type of table that sat in front of her desk, which actually looked more like where a judge would sit. It could easily seat forty angels.

Suzanne said, "Come now, you are here for good rea-sons, not bad. Let's move to a more pleasant sur-rounding."

Braeden didn't know how it could get any nicer. It was already so posh and fancy. Suzanne spread her wings and flew up thirty feet to where there was an open sitting area that one could only get to by flying. It could seat dozens of angels too, and it was much more homey. There were big, soft couches, green plants, some miniature palm trees, floating waterfalls, and clouds drifting around. He looked down and could see straight into the A.C.C.. He could see every monitor. Big sister is watching.

She smiled and said, "Yes, Braeden, that is exactly what we say."

Taylor and Morgan both found a big couch and stretched out. They were easily making themselves at home. Braeden sat down next to Suzanne in a large, circular chair that floated three feet off the ground. Suzanne sat in a big, floating, throne-like chair in the middle of the room. It looked like it swiveled around so that she could sit and look down into the A.C.C. It was apparent that she held discussions in this area quite a bit.

She said, "I am sure you are wondering about God being in my office, and also my new title. The announcement hasn't gone out yet, but I will go ahead and share with you. God promoted me to Archangel just a few minutes ago."

She smiled and continued, "Hello, Braeden. Welcome to my personal office in Internal Affairs. May you pray that this is the only time you come to visit. As you might have guessed, a lot goes on inside these walls, and unlike other parts of heaven, earth, and Angel Academy, this office is protected from the library for confidentiality purposes. On earth, this would be very similar to the court system, except it is for angels. As much as I'd like to think that all of my little angels are innocent, unfortunately that is not the case. Angels are given an extreme amount of power, including being able to bring human souls back to their mortal bodies, which, by the way, is not allowed. Once the soul has left the body, by Ordinance Title Section 11.18.14.1, under no circumstance is a human soul allowed to return to its prior vessel, on its own, or by angel interference.

Braeden liked her. Morgan feared her. Taylor was always a perfect little angel so he had nothing to fear.

Morgan remembered what had happened to her in this same office, and it wasn't a memory of sitting up in the lofty pillow-lounge room she was in now. No, that day had been a horrible day. And so, without any other evidence, Morgan thought she knew what had happened to Edwin, her longtime best friend. He probably broke a rule, likely against the Cupids, and he was being punished. Drake and Illana must have been witnesses to the crime. Marcia had to have been the victim. Morgan knew that if God was in the room, then Edwin's Angel Bracelet would be removed. Edwin, like Braeden, was a human mortal turned into an angel. Angels, like mortals, make mistakes. They sometimes make decisions that they do not have the right to make. Also, angels have accidentally, or purposefully, taken human lives... another crime in the angel world, carrying severe punishment if caught.

Braeden and his friends really wanted to know what happened to Edwin. Braeden didn't know Edwin personally, but he didn't want to have anything bad happen to him.

He asked, "What's happened to him? What is going to happen to him now?"

Suzanne took her glasses off and let them hang in front of her. She smiled and said, "What you would call a 'fallen angel' on earth, is an angel that has 'fallen from God's good grace', and there are a few ways that can happen."

Aaron M. Stephens, M.B.A.

14

You Bad Angel!

Morgan had heard the rules from Internal Affairs far too many times. She was pretty sure that Suzanne was not going to tell Braeden what Edwin did or what happened to him. That would just not be right. Instead, she started going over the Angel Laws. She waved her hand in the air and the first Angel Law appeared, "Always obey God".

"Do you know what happens to bad angels who do not follow God?" Suzanne asked Braeden.

"I am going to say it is more than a slap on the wrist and a scolding," Braeden answered.

"Cute, real cute," Morgan replied. Then to Taylor, "I like this one."

Suzanne said, "You are correct, it is more than just a slap and scolding. There are no three-strike rules. No second chances. You do what you are told and you don't ask questions. God maintains order and it is very important that his servants are always ready and willing to carry out his word." She continued, "In the next few years you will see some of the things that have happened; watch, witness, and pray that you never make the same mistakes."

Morgan got up out of her chair and floated over next to Braeden, expanding her giant wings. Her halo glowed white.

Suzanne reached over and touched two fingers to his forehead, similar to when Morgan had touched Braeden's forehead with one finger when he was reborn. Braeden saw utter chaos and destruction. He saw angels stealing "things"; balls of light, jewels, and a red ruby heart. He saw angels killing humans, whether they were under orders he did not know, but he was sure that if Suzanne was showing him, it wasn't something that they were supposed to do.

What seemed like an eternity lasted only moments.

Morgan and Taylor both knew what was going on, and had moved to the other side of Suzanne's lounge office. They looked down into the A.C.C. to watch a particular angel work. They were both watching Caden, peering into his monitor. His workstation was ten times the size of the other A.C.C. workstations, containing larger monitors, each with hundreds of little camera screens with humans on them. You could see hundreds of celebrities, royalty, and regular people; some of them had more than one Guardian, some of them had dozens.

Morgan and Taylor watched Caden's seemingly effortless work, as he notified angels and sent them to earth. His work was a much smaller scaled version of what Aaron did, monitoring prayers. Caden had several lower-ranking angels flying in and out, and back to him. Most of the time the prayers or concerns of the assets were very trivial; *"Be sure that we all pray for Kim & Kayne to get their brand new mansion,"* or, *"Let's really pray that I win that Academy Award Oscar even though I have like a million dollars already"*. These were the kinds of things that celebrities wished and prayed for. Morgan had always thought that their concerns were foolish, selfish, and undeserved, but she was an angel and it wasn't up to her what prayers or wishes came true for other angels' assets.

Taylor leaned over, touched his bracelet to Morgan's bracelet, and in an instant a flash of silver light encapsulated them into a private conversation. Suzanne and Braeden were literally in their own little world, and there was no reason to let anyone else in on their private thoughts.

Taylor looked intense; he had an idea of what might have happened to Edwin, but of course he wanted to know what Morgan thought, after all, she had been his best friend for thousands of years. She had also been Edwin's Guardian when Edwin was a mortal.

"Morgan, please tell me he wasn't stupid enough to think he could actually go on that crusade."

Morgan looked at Taylor and thought back, *"For ten thousand years he was bound and determined to get his hands on a Cupid's ruby heart to give to Minerva, so that she could become immortal. Like that wasn't going to go unnoticed."*

Morgan knew that everything she was thinking was private. Of course, God always knows all, but he wasn't going to interfere with her telling, or thinking, a story. Taylor had higher security clearance than Morgan did anyway.

Morgan knew Edwin long ago when he really *was* innocent and sweet. As a mortal, his name had been Jason, and by all means he had been a very good person. He volunteered at the hospital, reading stories to children and the elderly. He had been a father, a little league coach, a Sunday School teacher, and a role model to thousands of boys during his time on earth. Morgan had watched him his entire life, from birth all the way to death. He had been a very good citizen, rarely partaking in dangerous activities, and was a really "easy" asset to work with. Morgan had done such a great job protecting Jason, that she was quickly promoted and awarded additional assets to protect.

Morgan kept looking out of the large, glass atrium office windows into the A.C.C., and she thought to Taylor, "*I was afraid this was going to happen. He wasn't supposed to be my apprentice after he died as a mortal. He knew nothing, of course, just like Braeden. As a mortal, his love for Jessica was too strong, and it carried over to this side. He has been searching for Jessica ever since. He thought that if he became a Cupid it would help him find her. Of course, I never thought he would be successful.*

I am taking a wild stab in the dark that he kid-napped another Cupid, stole his or her ruby heart, and then broke the law by showing himself to a mortal to give her the heart."

Taylor also pretended just to be looking off in the distance, not "thinking" to Morgan. He was pretty shocked at what Morgan had thought to him, but he certainly couldn't let on that they were having this conversation. If what Morgan was saying was true, then it could be "game over" for Edwin.

Morgan thought, *"Of course, I am just speculating, and I have no idea what it is that he might have done, or if he broke any Angel Laws. Suzanne knows, God knows, and those other little Cupids know what happened. I don't think you or I are going to find out anytime soon."*

She reached over and touched her bracelet to Taylor's to break the link. Suzanne and Braeden were still in their little trance-like state. Morgan and Taylor had no idea how long Suzanne and Braeden were going to be "training", so they walked toward the edge of the platform and floated down.

Taylor said, "They're going to God's office next anyway, and we can't go. So we might as well let them be for now."

15

Official Angel Business

Morgan and Taylor kept walking in silence for a few minutes. Taylor was still letting it all sink in.

Taylor said, "I guess I am a little sheltered from living in the library all of the time. You have sparked my interest in Edwin, and now, Braeden. I think it's time to head back to the library to find out a little bit more about Edwin." He looked at Morgan with a very serious look.

She grinned and said, "Now you're talking."

He replied back, "We can't see what happened in

Suzanne's office, but we *can* see what Edwin did when he visited Venus, the home of the Cupids. Come on, let's go to the library." And in a flash, he twinkled, with Morgan following right behind.

They twinkled into the library, and instead of being at the grand entryway, they were in Taylor's office. His office resided at the top of the library, so he could peer down and see everything that was going on. It was truly a spectacular scene. Like in the Angel Command Center, he could look down to see who was where, and what they were doing. Even though they were just balls of light, it was clear as day who they were. On the wall was a cataloging system, and angels that were in a document would light up on the wall and then blink out. When an angel was active, all Taylor had to do was touch the lit-up name and the document would expand, showing exactly what was going on.

Taylor looked down at his white tuxedo and snapped his finger. A cloud of gold dust swirled around him and then he was in his more comfortable tunic and gold sandals. Morgan looked over at him and snapped her fingers too. A cloud of dust swirled around her and then she was in the same, simple tunic as when she met Braeden. Her hairstyle changed as well. No longer was it pulled up in a fancy style, but it was in a ponytail instead, which made her hair look really long. It stuck out from her head and trailed down her back.

"Love the outfits, love the shoes, love getting all dressed up, and sometimes enough is enough... but I love my sandals even more," she said, admiring her super-cute shoes.

Taylor chuckled as he glanced over from his desk. He was sorting through a bunch of floating documents in the air. It was clear that he was working, using his super-computer to find out what he was looking for. He mumbled, "Hmmm, now this is interesting."

Morgan had only been in Taylor's office once, and Taylor didn't have any working documents open at that time. She hadn't even known that he could access documents from his office. She said from across the room, sitting in a very plush, floating chair, "How interesting and convenient for you *not* to have to go into each document to find what you are looking for. I figured you had to go *into* them like everyone else." It was all very impressive the way he was in and out of documents, seeing things, taking notes, making little comments to himself while he worked. "Can anyone else access records like this?"

Taylor nodded and said, "There is limited access as to whom can access what, in this manner. Suzanne has a direct feed, just like I do, and of course you will never see Jefferson actually *in* the library."

Morgan said, "What is it you are doing right now? Are you actually working, or are you looking into Edwin?"

He replied back, "A little bit of both. Everything we need to know, or could possibly want to know is in this library, with exceptions of course. But what I am finding is a little more concerning than just a Cupid crime being committed. It looks like..." He paused for a moment and his A.B.L. lit up. A new voice came online and a puff of gold smoke appeared.

A tan, female angel with white hair appeared, and said, "I'm sorry, Taylor, that file is now locked and classified. Jefferson, from the Angel Council, is adding sensitive data to that file, and is currently editing it. I will notify you when it is available for you." The cloud of smoke vanished in a small poof.

Morgan said, "Who was that, and what was that about?"

He took a deep breath and replied back, "That was

Rachel. She is my administrative angel that oversees certain... activity. She works closely with Suzanne and Jefferson, reporting certain things back to me. I knew something was up and I was getting close... a little too close as I actually found his file. There is some serious stuff going on with him right now, and it's being recorded. We just can't see it until they are done with him."

His floating chair zipped across the room and he jumped out, flying twenty feet up in the air. Like Suzanne's office, his was very large, very tall, and you had to fly up really high to get anywhere. He landed on another level where there was another computer monitor system, similar to what he had below. Morgan jumped out of her chair too, and flew up to where Taylor was. She looked around, and like Suzanne's office, this was a much more comfortable sitting area.

Taylor walked over to the big monitor and touched a few buttons on the screen. Then he said, "Locate and identify angel Edwin."

The screen flashed a couple of times, and a virtual map appeared in front of him, showing the galaxy and what appeared to be Angel Academy and heaven. He waited a moment and then the virtual map flashed "INVALID ANGEL SEARCH" in large, red letters.

A second later, Rachel appeared again, in a poof of smoke. She said, "The subject previously known as Edwin has been decommissioned, and is no longer categorized as a Level One Angel."

"Holy Buckets!" exclaimed Taylor. "Rachel, do a search and tell me the location of the prior angel named Edwin."

Rachel replied, "Yes, sir, one moment please."

A virtual geographical map appeared again, and this time a red light blinked rapidly, and then slowly off in an area very far from heaven and earth. Rachel appeared in a poof of smoke and said, "The file you were previously accessing is now available for viewing. Shall I put it up on the screen?"

Taylor replied, "Yes, please, Rachel, thank you."

The large screen now showed Edwin. He was still bound with his halo on his wrists, but he no longer had wings and he was not wearing a tunic but was instead wearing a loincloth tied around his waist. He no longer had on an angel bracelet, and he looked like he had aged twenty or thirty years since they last saw him.

Rachel interrupted them and said, "The subject Edwin is awaiting transformation as punishment. Details are still not available as to what he did or where he will be sent."

Morgan finally chimed in and said, "Taylor, do you know what is going to happen to him?"

He took a deep breath and said, "No, I do not know for certain yet, but I am speculating that they are going to change him into something, and make him pay penance in a serving manner. He's not an angel; he's something else, but they are going to change him into something that can only do *good* things, and will no longer have the power to make choices that cause harm. It doesn't appear that he violated an Angel Law in regard to killing another angel. I think they are going to teach him a lesson. It will be a few hundred thousand years before he will be changed back."

Morgan seemed a little surprised. She had never been involved in an angel transformation. She hadn't even known that this could happen.

"What do you think will happen to him?" she said.

Taylor shook his head and said, "If he crossed a Cupid, I'd have to say he will spend the next few millennium as a fairy. And he won't be Edwin anymore. He'll be... Edwina."

Morgan looked at Taylor and said, "We have to save him."

16

God's Office

Meanwhile, Braeden and Suzanne were still in Suzanne's office. Braeden hadn't known what *two* fingers were going to do to him when they touched him. He had only known what it felt like when Morgan touched *one* finger to his forehead. That was scary. Did Angels do that on purpose? Could he scare someone that way also? He didn't really have any scary, demon-slaying experiences to share with anyone, so he decided he couldn't do it yet.

However, when Suzanne touched him, it was different. It didn't terrorize him like when Morgan did it, instead he got to see hundreds, no, thousands of images of things that happened in the past. Some of them were nice. Most of them were horrible.

Suzanne was there with him, and thought to Braeden, "*What you are witnessing is a crash course in angel history. This is much faster than you going into the library to find out everything. In what will seem like moments to us here, will have actually been years that have passed on earth.*"

Suzaane was right, it only seemed like minutes went by, and then, finally it was all over. He sat there in his chair, still in awe of all the raw information he just acquired. He finally said, "Do I have the power to heal a human, or other creatures?"

Suzanne smiled back and said, "Absolutely. Actually, when you were a human mortal you had the power to heal, you just did not know how to access that power."

Braeden asked her, "What other powers do I have? Can you tell me? I think I know, based on some of the things I saw, but it's not one hundred percent clear to me."

Suzanne said, "You have the power see into the short future and to go through time. You can see things as they happened. Time travel is risky business. You should *only* use this power if you are a Guardian and it means saving your asset. You have the power to enter into your asset's dreams to give them a message. If a human soul requests it, you may deliver messages to a human soul in heaven that has passed on. You have the power to take different shapes and forms. If, one day, you are promoted, you will have the power to be an Earth Angel and will be able to take the form of a human with all of your angel powers. You have the power to influence the weather; be careful where you aim those clouds. The Angels of Light do not like it when you cloud up their day."

She smiled. He wasn't sure if she was joking, but since he wasn't planning on using any clouds except for floating on, he was pretty sure he was okay.

"Now then, I do believe there is a certain someone who wants to talk with you. I promised I would take you up there as soon as we were done here," she said, reaching out her hand and grabbing his.

They both said, "God love me," and they turned into one little ball of light, a small orb that twinkled and sparkled with gold dust.

Suzanne thought to him, *"You can only enter God's office if he has given his permission. He is expecting you. Archangels are usually found in his office, along with Heralds. When you are in God's office, you will remain as a* ball of light. *Prepare yourself, for the awesomeness of God is pretty intense the first time. Human mortals cannot bear to see the direct presence of God, and as a result can only receive messages through Heralds. If a mortal were to be in God's presence and not be shielded, they would literally blow up. Not really a good thing."*

Braeden tried to think of an instance where someone said they were in the presence of God. Moses, Check. Noah, Check. Jesus, check. Okay, so there were some that had been in the presence of God but they didn't actually see him; they felt him. Suzanne thought, *"Do not expect to see God take the shape or form of a human or an angel. He can, of course, take any shape he wants."*

Within moments they were flying above the A.C.C., right over Aaron's halo, and up into God's office. Braeden felt a new sensation all over. It was different that anything he had ever felt before. Braeden looked around the office for a minute, and then he heard a deep, warm, baritone voice say, *"Hello, my son. I have been waiting for you."*

Braeden thought back, *"Hello, Father, I am ever so thankful to be in your presence. I am honored."*

Braeden glanced around the office and saw lots of

balls of light, Archangels, and in the center of the room he saw the uniquely warm, gold ball of light he had had a glimpse of earlier. It was the most glorious thing he had ever seen or felt. He loved the feeling. He knew that feeling was caused by God. He also saw a ton of little orbs there. They were white balls of light, not gold like the Archangels. He could only assume that they were the Heralds. He noticed that Suzanne was no longer with him. She must have just escorted him in so he could actually get into the office.

The deep baritone voice said, *"It is nice to see you again. I see you have made some slight adjustments since we last spoke. I do hope you are enjoying being an angel."*

Braeden replied back quietly, "Yes, thank you Father. I have learned a lot since we last spoke. I am amazed that Atlantis was saved."

God said to Braeden, *"Yes, there are times that I do step in. Actually, as you witnessed, I don't do any of the actual work. My angels are there to carry out my commands. Angels are extensions of myself, created as my second hands."*

Braeden said, "Why did you want to see me in your office, Father?"

God said, *"I have a gift for you. It is very important for your career as an angel. Up until now you have had to rely on your mentor and other angels to twinkle. You will need this very important skill if you are going to be successful."*

The big, gold ball that shone in front of him detached a smaller ball from it, and it floated toward Braeden until it touched his chest. His entire being was filled with love and light. He was now a glowing, gold sphere, just like God, instead of being a white orb. This was amazing and all he could do was think, *"Thank you, God"*.

If God could smile as a ball of light, he would have. Instead, he said, *"You are welcome, my son. Any time you want to go somewhere, you know what to say and think. You will be immediately transported anywhere in the universe, to any dimension. You cannot be harmed as an angel. You can inflict much harm, but only on my command. You do not have the power to make decisions, only to carry out orders. My orders. As long as you are true to my love, you will wield the power of the mighty Archangels. When you decide on an occupation come back to me, and I will award you with your last power."*

Braeden knew exactly where he wanted to go after that. He was filled with love and he said, "Thank you, Father. I love you." Then Braeden thought, "God *love me*," and heard, "*I am always loving you.*"

With a flash of bright light and a poof of gold dust, Braeden twinkled by himself for the very first time. He was on his way... or so he thought.

17

Oh, the Places You Will Go

There were all kinds of places that Braeden wanted to go. For the first time, he felt like he could do whatever he wanted as long as he did not break any Angel Laws. Atlantis? Back to earth? Angel Academy? The A.C.C.? The Garden of Angels? The home of the Cupids? Warrior Training Battlegrounds? No, he didn't want to go to any of those places just yet. Where he really wanted to go was Purgatory. He had read about it in books on earth, and heard scary stories as a mortal. God said that nothing could harm him... so why not?

He got a huge grin on his face and was just about

to utter the magic words when he heard, "Not so fast my little padawan," and behind him stood Morgan and Taylor. Morgan's arms were crossed and she said, "You didn't think you were going to get to go twinkling all over the universe unsupervised, did you?"

Braeden just stared back at her with a blank look on his face. "*Uh yeah, sort of, that was the idea,*" he thought to her.

"Seriously, Purgatory? Are you nutsoid, kiddo? Full-fledged angels don't even want to go there, and *that* is the first place you pick? You've got some issues, buddy." She rolled her eyes.

Taylor chuckled and said, "I can give you a glimpse into Purgatory without actually going in there. Hold that thought for now, little buddy."

Morgan replied, "I think it might be more fun for you to visit either the Warriors or the Guardians at this stage. After that, you can go visit those love hawks, the Cupids. Who knows, you might actually want to be one. You still need to forge a bow."

Braeden asked her with a strange look on his face, "Morgan, how many jobs have you held as an angel?"

He felt that it was a fair enough question. After all, if she was his mentor he should have a right to know what made her qualified.

She replied back, "Let's start walking toward the Guardians and I will tell you. It's kind of a long story. And technically, we do have eternity."

Braeden started walking and he noticed that they were in simple tunics again, despite being back in heaven. He snapped his fingers and a gold cloud of dust wrapped around him, changing his outfit to match his friends. They walked in silence for a little while before Morgan started her story. Braeden had learned by now that it was not a good idea to pressure Morgan for something when she wasn't ready. He could hear a harp playing "Amazing Grace" slowly and softly in the background.

Taylor looked up and said, "Bernice is playing God's favorite song right now. Even though I have heard it a hundred thousand times, I never get tired of hearing it."

Morgan smiled and said, "That is one thing, for sure, that we can all agree on. The music in heaven is just... heavenly. There are a few angels who are reborn on earth with their incredible musical ability.

Sasha created a television show just to promote those angels. Yes, believe it or not, they all started out in the Garden of Angels."

Braeden said, "Morgan, how did you get to be a Mentor or Training Angel? How do I earn my wings and halo?"

She replied, "You have to perform a good deed to get your wings. You have to save a human life to get your halo. Pretty simple, right? The more you do, the bigger your wings become. The more lives you save, the brighter your halo appears. Being a Guardian is the quickest and easiest way to do that, unless your mortal is a very safe, conservative human." She stopped walking, spread her wings, and shone her halo.

When looking at her without the white eyes and white fire, she looked very angelic. Before, Braeden couldn't see how big her wings were, and at the time, had no reference as to their size bearing any any importance. Her wings were magnificent and as large as an Archangel's. For a moment, Braeden wondered if Morgan was also secretly an Archangel but didn't tell him. If she was listening to his thoughts, she pretended like she didn't hear him.

"To be in a position like mine, you have to prove

to God on hundreds of occasions that you are worthy and a good, shining example of an Angel of the Lord," she said.

"So that is what you are, an Angel of the Lord?" he asked back.

"I *was* an Angel of the Lord, before I... stepped down," she said. She retracted her wings, and her halo slowly faded out.

Braeden asked, "Why does a Cupid have tiny wings?"

Morgan continued on, saying, "Cupids earn their wings when they get two mortals to fall in love. They are responsible for a lot of 'accidental' things that go on in mortal lives that put two people in the right place at the right time. They have other powers, too. Cupids were actually the original archers protecting heaven back in the day. Their arrows have evolved over time. All angels have to get their bows from a Cupid, including Angels of Death. Cupids can also take bows away."

Braeden was a little shocked that a Cupid had that kind of power. He imagined that they had different kinds of arrows that did different things.

Taylor, who was always good at hearing Braeden's questions, said out loud, "Oh, yes, you are right on. Tornadoes are actually caused by an Angel Arrow or a Demon Arrow, as are a lot of weather-related occurances."

Braeden asked, "How does an angel get all of these different kinds of arrows?" It seemed like a valid question.

Taylor responded back, "Angel Energy Dust."

Morgan said, "Okay, Braeden, where would you like to go?"

He smiled and said, "Can we go to Dog Heaven?"

Taylor grinned and Morgan smiled. She said, "Sure, that would be a fantastic idea!"

Braeden said, "Great... uh, where is it?"

Taylor and Morgan both said at the same time, "Just over the Rainbow Bridge," and they pointed over in the distance. He hadn't noticed it before, but then again he wasn't looking.

Taylor said, "You will like Dog Heaven. Sara, the Senior Angel, has one of the best jobs. Who wouldn't love being around dogs and puppies all of the time?"

Morgan smiled, laughed, and said, "Get ready for the best day of your life!"

18

Dog Heaven

Taylor, Morgan, and Braeden had begun to walk toward the Rainbow Bridge when Braeden heard another familiar voice, Aleona.

"Really? Dog Heaven? You are one of the few new angels to even acknowledge that it is even here," said Aleona.

Taylor laughed and said, "Oh, you wanna hear where big boy Braeden wanted to twinkle to first? Purgatory! Only the bravest angels ever go there."

Braeden piped up and said, "I want to be a brave angel! Can we please go to Purgatory?"

Morgan snorted and said, "You see? I told you he was nutsoid."

Aleona nodded in agreement with Morgan.

Aleona said "Braeden, you really don't want to go there. That is the one place that is super-depressing. If you really want to see it, go there with Zoltan, he is the Senior Angel for Warriors, he will keep you safe." Taylor had never been to Purgatory, and Morgan had only been there once. Aleona had been there several times, and she didn't like it at all.

She said, "Everything is so, so dark, and being an Angel of Light, I am not welcome there."

Braeden decided that a future trip with a Senior Warrior Angel sounded like a good idea. He couldn't be hurt but that didn't mean that other things couldn't happen. They walked a little further, and Aleona walked next to Braeden.

She caught up with him and said, "Braeden, why do you want to go to Dog Heaven?"

He didn't say anything at first, and then said, "I remember once, when I was a kid, I had this little dog. It was a miniature pincher and I loved her to pieces. She lived a very long life, longer than most dogs because I fed her raw chicken and organic food. She was the best thing that happened to me, and when she died I was so sad. I cried for days. But I knew that one day I would get to see her again. My mom promised me that, one day, I could go to Dog Heaven to see my little Min-Pin. So, here I am, and of all the places I could go, this is number two on the list. Morgan said that I can't see human souls in heaven, but she never said anything about dog souls."

Morgan and Taylor were walking behind, quietly listening to Braeden talk. Morgan was more interested than she normally was, and she hopped along and flew to catch up with the other two. Taylor was right behind.

"Say, Braeden! Tell me more about your little puppy dog. Do you remember his name?" Morgan asked.

Braeden stopped for a moment and shook his head. "You know, that is the one thing I just can't remember and I don't know why. I can *see* her; I can close my eyes and almost feel her. I can feel the love that she would shower me with every day as she would kiss my face... but I can't remember her name. Weird."

He walked a little more, not saying anything. Morgan looked over at Taylor with a strange look on her face.

Taylor chimed in and said, "Well, she certainly will be happy to see you. Animal souls are a little different, as they will remember you even if you are in a different form. It's amazing. Their love, like God's love, is unconditional."

Braeden smiled, and then said, "When I was a little boy, I think like five or six years old, my little dog saved my life. I can remember it like it was yesterday. We were playing in the forest and I was running after my dog. I think she saw a squirrel or something because she got all excited and was barking and pulling on her leash really hard. I remember because it was a really sunny day, and then all of the sudden, out of nowhere, there were dark clouds, and then thunder and lightning, but no rain. I thought it was strange that there was so much thunder. A lightening bolt came out of the sky and hit a tree next to me."

Morgan stopped him and said, "Wait a second, Braeden. Do you remember anything else that was strange or peculiar about that day?"

He stopped for a second and said, "Yes, I remember that there was a very large, dark cloud above me and it was only above *me*." He continued his story, "Then, all of the sudden, it got really, really dark. The wind started to blow really fast and a tree branch hit me in the head from the deadly wind. When I woke up I was in the hospital. My mom was there, and said that my dog ran home and made my mom come to find me. She said that she knew something was wrong when she couldn't find me, and she prayed to God for help. And just like that, my little dog ran home and barked nonstop at her. She knew I had been playing with my dog, and knew something was wrong. She ran after my dog and found me lying unconscious next to a burning tree. Yes, my little dog saved my life that day."

Aleona said, "Wow, Braeden, that is an amazing story. I am excited to meet your little dog."

Hearing Braeden's story sparked something in Morgan. She didn't think it was possible, but for the first time she considered that she had known Braeden as a human mortal. She didn't like this little "coincidence," and needed to talk to God. Morgan then said, "Hey, you guys go play with the dogs for a little while. There is something that I need to tend to back at the A.C.C.." In a flash, she twinkled, and there was just a small pile of Angel Dust where she had stood.

They walked a little further in silence before they came to the "Rainbow Bridge." At the bridge was another angel, blocking it, standing behind a silver gate. There was a sign that said, "Please encourage our playful puppies to stay in Dog Heaven. Thank you. God." The Rainbow Bridge was nothing like what Braeden had thought it was going to be. He actually thought it was going to be a band of different colored lights that they would walk, or float over. Nope, nothing like that at all. This was a *huge* bridge, and it looked like it was made out of bricks. It was half a mile wide and went for what looked like miles before getting to the other side. There was nothing under the bridge but clouds and blue sky. The bricks were an iridescent color that changed constantly, making the bridge shimmer and shine. It was breathtaking.

At the other side, a wonderland of green grass could be seen, with meadows, fields, streams, and trees everywhere. It was just beautiful. Braeden could see why it was heaven for dogs. The angel standing at the gate smiled. He was handsome, and like Suzanne, appeared much older than he was.

He said, "Hello, Braeden. Welcome to Dog Heaven. My name is Jeremiah. If you have any past loved ones here, they will know you instantly. It's one of the really cool things about Dog Heaven. Oh, yes, and dogs don't eat or drink in heaven, just like angels and humans, so don't try to feed my dogs."

He pressed a button and the silver gate opened, allowing the three of them to walk inside. He pushed the button again and it closed behind them. Directly in front of them was an invisible, shimmering, see-through door. There were some puppies directly on the other side. Jeremiah pushed a different button and the door opened up, ten feet from the ground. The three angels had to float up to get over to the other side. Then they gently floated down, and immediately all three of them were showered with kisses from dozens of dogs and puppies. Braeden was laughing and giggling so much that he almost forgot about his own dog. He pictured his dog in his mind, and then he saw her. She came bouncing up over the meadow, running as fast as she could. Braeden finally remembered his dog's name.

"DELILAH!"

Taylor and Aleona stood there watching the little puppy run across the green meadow, bouncing and barking all at the same time. Tears streamed down Aleona's angelic face.

She said, "I just get really happy when they finally get to be with their little puppies."

Unfortunately for Morgan, she was standing in the A.C.C. arguing to Aaron that she needed to see God. If she had only stayed at Dog Heaven for just a few more minutes, she would have heard Braeden shouting out his dog's name, and it would have answered her question. The question that was burning in her heart right now was, "Did God allow her first asset to also be her apprentice? Was this torture or a reward?"

19

Oh Jesus! Air Force One Under Attack!

Aaron sat in his floating chair at his large, see-through desk, overseeing the A.C.C.. He listened quietly with his hands clasped as Morgan began to plead her case. His monitor systems were pretty impressive, and unlike Suzanne, he and God were the only ones who could see into them. Nothing and no one, including the library, could see into God's office.

Morgan had to get in there to see God. She knew the rules: "No admittance without expressed interest, invitation, or escort of a Herald." Aaron pointed to the sign above him above the door, about fifty feet up. Unfortunately, in the past there had been some really touchy stuff going on in there, and letting the wrong information into the wrong hands had proved deadly.

Aaron said to Morgan, "Look, I was in the office at the time that God said, '*The time has come to destroy all of my creations except for one of each species, male and female. I shall purify the earth and cleanse it with the heavenly rains. Angels shall cry endlessly onto the earth.*' If the wrong angel knew of this, Morgan, it would cause utter chaos in heaven *and* on earth. As you know, when it just kept raining, no one really paid much attention. So anyway, Morgan, you know I love you like a daughter. We've been around together for a really, *really* long time. You have experienced utter destruction, even a civilization or two destroyed if I remember correctly. I watched it all from my chair. I happen to know for a fact that, right now, God is actually busy in his office at the moment, and will be back online shortly."

A puff of gold glitter smoke appeared and Aaron's A.B.L. lit up. A lovely, Asian, female angel appeared. Her hair was black with white and purple highlights, and was tied up off of her neck. She wore a gold headset, had very long eyelashes, and was very beautiful. She had on a white scarf tied around her neck.

Aaron looked at Morgan and said, "Excuse me for just a moment." A see-through, invisible shield went up between he and Morgan, giving him exclusive privacy.

He looked over at the angel in the dust cloud and said, "Report status, Karyn."

"I have been spying on the angel formerly known as Edwin, as requested, Sir. I instructed Rachel to tell Morgan that it was Jefferson who had the file locked. Rachel is standing by, awaiting instructions to report to Taylor. What shall I do, Sir?" she said.

Aaron looked over at Morgan, who was peering down into the A.C.C. at Caden again. Caden had the President of the United States on his giant monitor, watching him and his cabinet in Air Force One. On other monitors there were images of the outside of the plane, and there were dozens of Guardians and Warriors flying as invisible escorts to the fighter jets that also surrounded it. Over each of the fighter planes were additional Guardians flying close by. It was a really spectacular sight to see the angels in formation.

As she was watching, a bright yellow light flashed in different sections of the A.C.C.. Different screens were giving alerts — some priority, others full alert. Angels responded quickly, pressing buttons on their screens, touching their headsets, and dispatching additional angels. Caden's section was going off like fireworks, so she leaned in closer to get a better look.

Aaron was interested to see what was going on as well, and pressed a button on his screen. Caden's screen was now also visible on Aaron's screen, and he could see and hear real-time as if he were standing right there.

He looked over at Karyn and said, "Inform Rachel that the file has been updated with new information, including the identity and location of the former angel known as Edwin. *Ever* so thankful, Karyn." She smiled and poofed out in a cloud of gold glitter dust.

Aaron lowered the privacy shield and Morgan came back over, so that she could see and hear what the ruckus was all about. It appeared that, above the President's giant Boeing, there were hundreds of

Angels of Death, silently flying along. Many of them carried swords, staffs, spears, and other large weapons. They all had shields, and their wings were black.

A few thousand kilometers away, terrorists were planning to attack Air Force One. Aaron could hear the voices of the terrorists on their cell phones and radios, speaking in a foreign language that Morgan didn't recognize. She was confused; she knew every language.

Aaron said, "They are talking in an ancient dialogue code in fourteen different, randomly-changing languages. There! That was Vietnamese; that was French, that was part Russian, that was Spanish, there was some Chinese. They are doing it to hide their true identity. It's very difficult to follow."

Morgan said, "Do you know who they are?"

Aaron looked at her and said, "Well, I wouldn't be very good at my job if I didn't."

He pressed a button on the lower right-hand side of his screen, which she could not previously see. It enlarged and was now filling up the entire half of his screen.

"This is the man who is talking. You don't recognize him. No one does. He is no one right now. But if he pulls this off, he will go down in history. This is something that takes a high priority due to the passengers on board. I have known about this event for some time now. Teegan, a Time Angel, came to me about this about twenty years ago, to report the catastrophic result it had on earth."

Aaron didn't appear to be phased one little bit.

Caden, on the other hand, looked like he was going to lose it. If the President of the United States went down on his watch, there would be heaven to pay, like a demotion to Angel Dust cleanup crew. It was almost as if Aaron sort of enjoyed watching Caden, to see what he was going to do next.

Morgan couldn't believe that Aaron wasn't going to do anything to help. Morgan could see into the short, but distant, future, and she saw what Caden saw… the President's plane and its protectors shot out of the skies, thousands jumping out of parachutes, only to be shot at by other planes. Explosions, fire, and smoke everywhere. She saw a dead military official floating down in a parachute and her soul being carried off to heaven by her Guardian.

She had seen a lot of horrific things in the past, but this was just sad.

Then, something happened that she had never seen before. A flock of angels twinkled in everywhere, filling the sky with a gold, wispy dust, eventually covering it. Magically, things began to rewind. It was as if time itself was going backwards. Morgan stared in complete awe.

Aaron pushed a button and the entire screen went blank. He smiled, and said to Morgan, "Well now, I do believe a certain apprentice is awaiting your return."

She couldn't believe that Aaron would not show her what was going to happen to the President of the United States. She floated over to the edge of the platform and looked down. Everything was normal. It was as if nothing had happened. She went back to Aaron and said, "Um, what just happened?"

He said, "My dear, if I got all worked up every time something like this happened, I'd never get anything done. I didn't get anxious like you did because I have already seen the outcome, several outcomes actually. I talked it over with God and Teegan, and we sent

Time Angels to change the past. The angels in the Royal Sentry think that they just did a simulation."

Morgan had thought that she knew it all. Well, most of it anyway. She said, "I have never heard of a Time Angel. I think you are making it up."

He looked back at her and said, "Making it up? Like this was a piece of fiction? No, no, my padawan. There are many things that have happened here in heaven, and in the A.C.C., since you last worked a desk."

Aaron's A.B.L. lit up and a gold puff of smoke appeared. A very handsome, but older male, appeared. He had dark hair and beautiful eyes. It was like looking into a galaxy nebula. He said, "Hello, Aaron, so nice to see you again. I have been on earth, and many human souls have been praying to me to ask Father to save them. May I go in and see him?"

Aaron smiled and said, "Of course, Jesus, like you have to ask."

Jesus smiled and said, "Love ya, brother!" and he blinked out.

Morgan said, "That was Jesus? Really? He always looks different when I see him. The only thing that was the same were his amazing eyes. The last time that I saw him he had silver hair... same eyes, same smile. I thought you said God was busy."

Aaron said, "Seriously? That was Jesus. I think he just likes to pop in and say hi. You know, back in the day we were quite close. I consider him a best friend and a brother. Now then, you wanted to know more about Time Angels, huh? Well, I suppose it couldn't hurt just to *tell* you about them."

20

Time Angels

Aaron snapped his fingers and another floating chair appeared. "Please, Morgan, sit," he said.

Morgan sat quietly in the floating chair, awaiting Aaron's explanation. She was literally hanging onto every word, wanting to know about Time Angels. For all she knew, she might even want to *be* one.

Aaron said, "Morgan, you are bound to secrecy regarding what I am about to tell you. Changing time and altering the time continuum for humans can have catastrophic effects. Abuse of this power has resulted in cities crumbling to the ground, sinking below the seas to become giant homes to sea creatures. Some demons even know of this power, and want to use it in an evil way. While it has never been recorded, human civilization has faced extinction numerous times. God and the Angel Council have altered time for the sake of saving the world, at least earth. There are other planets and civilizations that have also had time changed to save their species."

Aaron tapped his bracelet and it lit up. He thought of whom it was he wanted to talk with, and then suddenly, a poof of gold glitter and a new, male face appeared in the cloud of smoke. He appeared to be older than Morgan, almost in his thirties. He was attractive, and had dark gold hair instead of blond. He had a square jaw and looked very serious. Aaron touched his wrist again, and this time the angel in the cloud of dust appeared on Aaron's big monitor.

Aaron said, "Hello, Justin. When you have a moment I would like you to come to my office, please. *Ever* so thankful," and then Justin poofed into gold dust.

Morgan asked, "Who was that?"

Aaron replied, "That was Justin, and if you hadn't been certain, yes, he is a Time Angel. They don't hang out in Angel Academy, or anywhere in heaven for that matter. They exist on a different astral plane, as to not interfere with normal daily business. They are only called upon in times of great need. They can only be dispatched by my command."

Morgan replied, "Wait a second. I can go back in time and see shortly into the future, but I have never been able to change anything in the past, only alter the future. What do Time Angels do most of the time? What makes a Time Angel so special that they aren't wiped out when they travel through time?"

Aaron said, "Well, like here in the A.C.C., they monitor all cultures, listen to prayers, and they see into the very distant future with all possible outcomes. They have a power that allows it."

Suddenly, there was an explosion of white and silver glitter dust and a flash of light, and there stood Justin, Time Angel, handsome as ever. He was tall, standing at seven feet. He, like Guardians, were very large in size, had large muscular figures, and appeared to be very strong. He wore an identical tunic that all the angels wore. He, however, had on white boots that went up to his knees. He also had two thick, gold wrist bands at least two inches in size. He did not wear a bracelet, but his wrist bands acted in the same fashion. He also did not wear a nametag, but instead had it embroidered onto his tunic: "Justin, Time Angel".

When he appeared, his large, impressive wings were extended, however they did not bear the usual marking of angel wings. They were invisible. You could make out the shape and you could definitely see that they were there, but they shimmered, like a mirage on the highway. He left them fully spread but relaxed. He didn't dissolve his wings into Angel Dust like other angels did. His halo was the same in the manner that it shone and shimmered. Morgan sat there, silently staring at this new angel she had never seen before, other than on the monitor a few moments ago.

Aaron was sitting at his desk when his A.B.L. lit up again. Aaron pushed a button on his screen, and an angel appeared on the large screen instead of in a cloud of dust on his arm. It was Karyn's angelic face that lit up the large screen. Aaron pushed another button and the invisible privacy shield went up between he the other angels.

"Report status, Karyn?"

Karyn looked concerned and it came through in her voice. "I'm sorry to interrupt, Sir, but I have detected some irregular activity in the Atlantis Sector. Unauthorized entry. Warrior Angels are preparing to investigate. I can't get through to Cameron or Desiree. I'm afraid that Queen Andromeda is also unresponsive." She awaited instruction. She blinked her long eyelashes twice and smiled.

Morgan and Justin were very interested in what was going on behind that privacy shield. She had all kinds of questions for Justin about time travel, but this was now twice that Aaron had put up the shield to talk to this mysterious angel. She asked Justin, "Do you know who that Asian angel is?"

He replied back, "Yes and no. I don't know her name. I know what she does though, she works for Aaron. She has come to our dimension before. I have also seen her fighting demons on earth. She is one *stealth* bomber, if I ever saw one. I honestly don't know what kind of angel she is, or what her official duty is. She's not a Guardian or a Warrior, for sure. She's pretty enough to be a Cupid."

Morgan's A.B.L. lit up and it was Taylor. A cloud of gold dust appeared and she was looking directly at him. He said, "Hi, Morgan, I just got word from Rachel that she knows the location of the file I was looking for earlier. When you get a chance, can you come back to Dog Heaven to watch over Braeden? I would let you into my office to get the file, but, as you know, I am the only one who can get in." The cloud of dust disappeared as it slowly littered the floor with more Angel Dust.

Morgan looked back at Justin and said, "What was she doing with the Time Angels?"

Justin replied back, "I don't know. She usually only works with Teegan. I just know *of* her. When I asked Aaron who she was, he told me to mind my own business."

Aaron was still sitting in his chair, not paying attention to Morgan and Justin.

Karyn said, "Sir, information has been delivered successfully to Taylor, via Rachel." She paused. "Sir, I have activity going on in another sector of the galaxy. Whatever happened in Atlantis is now causing problems elsewhere. May I dispatch to investigate?"

Aaron nodded and said, "Yes, send a scout and report back. *Ever* so thankful, Karyn." He pushed a button and she blinked off the screen. He took a deep breath and said, "What in God's great universe could possibly be going on now?"

His A.B.L. went off again. "*What now?*" he thought. He pressed another button and this time it was Desiree on the big screen. She looked distressed. She was beautiful with dark hair that was pulled up in a fancy, braided hairdo.

She said, "Greetings, Aaron. I am sorry to disturb you, but there has been a break *into* Atlantis. We were always afraid it was something wanting to get out, we never really thought of something trying to get *in*."

Aaron said, "Good God, can it get any worse?"

Desiree said, "Yes, actually it can. Queen Andromeda has been kidnapped and is being held for ransom."

He shook his head and said, "Really?"

Desiree replied back, "Yes, *really*, really. And here is the bad news."

Aaron couldn't believe there was even more bad news after this. What could possibly be worse than an interstellar galactic war over the Queen of the Mermaids?

Desiree said, "Brace yourself for this one. Four dragons have been stolen along with a Chimera *and* the Cracken."

21

Zoltan, Warrior Command

Morgan quickly found herself both needing, and wanting, to be in more than one place at a time. She needed to get back to Dog Heaven so that Taylor could find out what happened to Edwin. She was bound and determined to save him before it was too late. She was going to find out who that Asian angel was that Aaron was talking with if it was the last thing she did. Surely Taylor knew something about her. If Taylor had his own assistant, Rachel, it would stand to reason that Aaron would have an assistant too. But why all of the secrecy? Morgan had a feeling that Aaron knew dozens of secrets about all kinds of things. For example, who knew that he was best buds with the big Jay C.?

She looked over at Justin and said, "As much as I would love to hear about Time Angels, I really have to get back to my apprentice. Raincheck?"

She smiled at him and he said, "Sure, hit me up on the A.B.L., now that you know how to find me. I will always be able to find you." The two of them both twinkled, leaving more gold Angel Dust.

With a flash of light, Morgan was out of there and standing in front of Jeremiah at the enormous Rainbow Bridge. She couldn't see Braeden, as he was on the other side of the bridge.

Jeremiah came over and said with a sneer, "My, my, my, what do we have here?"

Morgan blurted back, "I am an Angel of the Lord, and I request passage to Dog Heaven, most graciously, thank you."

He looked at Morgan and then said, "Welcome, Morgan."

He opened the silver door and she walked in. She walked slowly until she hit the invisible wall. She looked up and then floated across. Jeremiah really wasn't very friendly, but that was okay. Morgan was looking for Nathan and Taylor. She walked for a little while, passing all kinds of dogs and puppies. This went on for a while, and she wondered if she was going to find them at all.

She stopped for a moment and said out loud, "Now, why did I think I was looking for Nathan? I haven't said his name in ages!"

She tapped on her A.B.L. and said, "Braeden," and with a poof of smoke, he was there. "Where are you?" she asked. "Hold on." And POOF. More gold smoke, and she was instantly standing next to them. "Amazing how that works."

Braeden had a small dog in his arms. He was hugging it and kissing it.

Aleona said, "You can stay here as long as you like, but they can't leave."

Taylor looked up and saw that Morgan had finally arrived. He said to her, "Where have you been for so long? We were starting to get worried... okay, *I* was getting worried. Braeden and Delilah have been having a great time over yonder." Taylor smiled and in a flash he was a cloud of dust, back at the library.

Braeden looked up, gave his puppy a hug, and said, "Where did Taylor go?" He looked around and then down at the Angel Dust.

Morgan said, "Work. Are you done yet? You still need to go see some more Senior Angels. I know I said we have eternity, but there are things that I want to do sometime in the next decade."

"Leaving so soon, Morgan? I haven't seen you in this part of heaven since.... gosh, how long *has* it been?"

The three of them turned around to see a beautiful angel that had to be Sara, the Senior Angel. Sure enough, there Sara stood, radiating love and joy. She had dozens of all kinds of little puppies at her feet. She had long, blonde hair that had dark streaks of brown, black, and even red in it. It was very straight and hung down to her waist. Her tunic was different than the ones Braeden had seen. She was wearing white pants with black boots. She had on a gold nametag that matched her bracelet.

She saw Braeden looking at her pants and said, "If I had on what you have on, my legs would be a disaster with dogs and puppies always jumping up on me."

Sara looked back over at Morgan and narrowed her eyes, pursed her lips, and then said, "Hmmm, Morgan... *who* was it you that were looking for in Dog Heaven all those years ago? You have never been mortal, so there wouldn't be a puppy that *you* had loved."

Morgan knew exactly who it was that she had been looking for in Dog Heaven many, many years ago. She knew it, Sara knew it. Why was Sara being like this?

Braeden was still holding Delilah tightly, but she was squirming like she knew Morgan, and wanted to kiss her.

Morgan said back, cooly, "Sara, I have no idea what you are talking about. Once, when I was a Guardian, I promised my asset that I would go to Dog Heaven to make sure his puppy made it here after it died. I did; it was here, and then I left. End of story."

Sara reached over and touched her bracelet to Morgan's bracelet, and said, "Are you sure it isn't *this* dog, here in Braeden arm's, that you were checking on?" Then she broke the connection.

It happened so fast that Braeden didn't even know they had "thought" to each other.

Sara smiled, and in an innocent, sweet voice like sugar, said, "Of course it is."

Braeden looked up and said, "Of course it is what?"

Sara said, "Of course it is the end of the story."

Morgan ignored her and said to Braeden, "Now, my little padawan, some really fun exciting stuff is going on, and as much as I would love to hang out with you here in Dog Heaven, I am sure you'd rather go on a ride-along, wouldn't you? Wouldn't you rather go learn how to forge a sword out of Angel Dust?"

Braeden looked over at Sara and said, "Thank you so much for playing with us. Delilah really likes you. Seeing her and hugging her was a dream come true. Hearing her thoughts in Dog Heaven was the best part. Today is the best day of my life... death... whatever it is."

Sara reached over and hugged Braeden and Delilah.

Braeden handed Delilah over to Sara. She held her and said, "Don't worry, little Braeden, we will be right here in Dog Heaven. Come back as often as you like. We're just down the happy trail, beyond the meadow of contentment, just after the Rainbow Bridge."

The three little teenage-looking angels turned and walked back toward the Rainbow Bridge. Tears were streaming down Braeden's and Aleona's faces. Morgan looked over and felt the sadness that Braeden looked like he felt. She reached over and grabbed Braeden's hand. She thought, "*Why so sad, my little Angel?*"

He looked over at her and thought, "*I'm not sad, I'm happy. I was sad and happy when I could hear Delilah in my head. She said she has been sitting by the happy trail for a really long time waiting for me, and that I took longer to get here than she thought I would. She also said she was sorry she was the one who got me killed. But she didn't get me killed. I don't remember how I died. I know my puppy did not kill me.*"

Morgan said, "Did she say what happened or how you got killed?"

He shook his head and said, "No, she said she

promised God that she would never bring it up because it is very sad. And there is no place for sadness here, only happy thoughts. And then she licked my face and gave me a kiss and I forgot all about it."

Aleona wiped away a tear and said, "I have never really loved dogs until just now."

Braeden said, "Where are we going now?"

Morgan replied, "We need to pick up Taylor and then we will be on our way. Braeden, can you twinkle there yourself?"

He smiled and said, "*Now* I can!" He closed his eyes and thought of the library and said, "God love me" and again heard back, "*I am always loving you.*"

With a flash of light, he was standing in Taylor's office with Morgan, Aleona, Taylor, and a new angel Braeden had never seen before. This new angel was taller than the rest of them, and stood at probably seven feet. He was talking to Taylor and he was much older than the rest of them. If they had been on earth, they would look like a father and a bunch of kids. His wings were fully extended, as if to shield their conversation.

This new angel didn't have any hair, like it had all

been shaved off, and he looked mean. He had thick, gold bands on each wrist. He did not have a gold bracelet, just the arm bands. He also had a tattoo symbol on his right, outside bicep that looked like some sort of a winged insignia. He wasn't wearing a tunic, but instead had on a white, leather-type of strap that formed an X across his chest. In the middle of the X was the same insignia that was on his arm. Under it, his muscular chest and six-pack abs could be seen. Like Drake, he had a white, smaller version of a tunic. He had very large, muscular legs and had on white boots that went just over his ankles.

When he turned, Braeden could see a teeny, tiny, gold nametag on the right of his chest. It read "Zoltan, Senior Warrior Angel". It looked small on him only because he was so large. Zoltan was wearing a white mask that only covered his eyes, like he was a superhero or something. Braeden imagined that when his eyes were all white, like the time when Morgan got all holy on him, that Zoltan would be a very frightening site.

Zoltan laughed in a deep, bass voice, and said to Braeden, "Hi, Braeden. Yes, you better believe that I can scare the wits out of someone."

Braeden was excited. He knew that Zoltan was going to teach him how to make a sword, *and* he was also the one who would escort him through Purgatory.

Morgan looked over at Taylor and he gave her an approval nod, letting her know that he had found out where the angel previously known as Edwin was located.

Zoltan reached his hand out to shake Braeden's. Braeden grabbed it and shook it. He felt something new with this Warrior Angel. He felt a sudden surge of energy like he had never felt before. It ripped though him like shock waves, filling him with a renewed sense of purpose. He liked this new feeling.

"Come," said Zoltan, "the library is no place for Warriors to hang out. We must return to our home planet where you can *really* experience what we are like." He looked at the other party members.

Morgan said, "We know where it is. We will be there in just a few... I need to talk with Taylor and Aleona about something important."

Zoltan nodded, and in a flash of light and a cloud of gold glitter, exploded into a small pile of dust.

22

The Temptress of Seduction

Aaron sat in his floating chair wondering what he should do next. *A break-in into Atlantis? Why would someone want to steal dragons? Who even knows they are there?*

A warm, familiar, male voice behind him said, "Angels and Demons have broken into Atlantis. The missing Angel Bracelet that was stolen centuries ago has been activated by Angel Dust and used in the crime." Aaron turned and saw Jesus sitting in another floating chair next to him. Aaron reached out his hand and Jesus gave him a knuckle bump.

Aaron said, "*Ever* so grateful to have you here, now of all times. I really needed someone to talk this out with," he paused, "Any suggestions would be much appreciated."

Jesus calmly said, "Well, it appears that Morgan and Taylor are determined to save Edwin. And we certainly do want that to happen. Zoltan and Aleona are also good choices. However, to make things a little more interesting, a Cupid should also join their group."

Aaron said, "I know for a fact that all of the Cupids are overworked and unavailable. There are never enough to go around, and the world desperately needs love."

Jesus said, "Well, there *is* another Cupid that would make herself available if I asked her."

He touched his bracelet and a poof of gold dust appeared, displaying a very familiar face to Aaron. It was Ashley, a rogue angel, previously a Cupid. Aaron hadn't seen her in over a hundred years.

She glanced over and saw Aaron, and her smile quickly faded away. Instead, she looked back over at

Jesus and said, "Hello, handsome. *Ever* so grateful to see you!"

Jesus cleared his throat and said, "Ahem, would you mind joining us?"

In a flash, Ashley was standing in front of them, beautiful as ever. Ashley had long, dark brown hair with streaks of blond in it. She had it pulled up in a thick, long ponytail that hung down to her waist. She looked nothing like an angel, and wore a tight, white, latex outfit with gloves that went up to her elbows. She had on tall, high-heeled boots that went all the way up to her thighs. She still wore a gold Angel Bracelet on her left arm. The top of her outfit was tight, and for an angel, a little too revealing, which made her very "busty". Around her neck and suspended in the air was a red ruby heart worn as a pendant, just like Illana's. Ashley, however, did not glow like Illana, and lacked that certain "flare" that the other Cupids had. She carried a gold crossbow in her right hand. She was also wearing a see-through, white cape that covered her shoulders and the place where her wings should have been. It floated gracefully around her as she moved.

"A rogue Cupid? Really? That's your answer?" said Aaron.

Jesus smiled and waved his hand in the air, and a cloud of gold dust swirled around Ashley. Suddenly, she was dressed in a simple, silver and white tunic, except it was longer than the standard issued tunics, reaching down to her knees and looking more like a dress. She still had on her long gloves and her big, white, high-heeled boots. Her floating cape was also gone.

Aaron responded, "If you are going to be a part of the team, you have to at least *look* the part." A small ball of white light appeared in the palm of his hand. He tossed the small ball at her, saying, "You might need this." The light ball exploded into a halo that she caught on the tip of her crossbow. "No one will believe you are a Cupid if you are missing that."

She put it on her head, and all of the sudden she lit up in a soft glow. She said, "Ahh, now *that* feels good. It's been a long time." She bowed her head and said, "Ever so thankful."

Stretching her back, an invisible glow of small Cupid wings formed there. She said, "I haven't seen those in a long time either. Now, what exactly am I doing here, and why did you just give me back my halo?"

Jesus looked at Ashley and said, "Aaron and I need you to go on an important mission. There is a group of little angels that are off to save an innocent from doom. Your job is to infiltrate their trust and lead them to where we tell you. You are to teach one of the newest, youngest angels about Cupids, without influencing his emotions."

"What else?" she snapped.

He looked at her sternly and she looked down. She said, "Apologies, my King. May I also inquire what other services I can fulfill for thee?"

Jesus said, "You are to reveal this to no one. You will report your progress and status back to Aaron on a regular basis. Your goal is to help Braeden earn his wings."

She did not look up, but asked, "And how shall I be integrated into the group, Sir?"

He said, "I will have Karyn escort you to the Warrior Planet where the group is heading now."

Aaron reached over, touched his A.B.L., and thought of Karyn. She appeared in a poof of gold glitter dust. "Karyn, please report to my office," he said, and she was there in a flash, standing next to Ashley.

Karyn was a short little angel. She wore a simple, white tunic but instead of big, white boots she had on small, high-heeled boots that only went up to her calves. She still had on her white, silk scarf but she also wore white, leather gloves that just covered her A.B.L..

She looked at Ashley but didn't say anything.

Ashley looked her up and down and said, "Hello. You must be Karyn. I'm Ashley. It is nice to meet you."

Karyn narrowed her eyes, looking at her through her long, dark eyelashes. She finally said, "Yes. I know who you are. And I am well aware of *what* you are."

Ashley didn't seem at all offended by Karyn's remark. Evidently, she was used to such cold treatment. She smirked and said, "You know, sweetheart, it looks like we are going to be pals for the next few decades, so can you lose the attitude?"

Karyn ignored Ashley, looking at Aaron instead, and said, "Sir, what is my assignment?"

Aaron looked at both of the two beautiful angels standing in front of him and said, "Your mission," he looked directly at Ashley, "*should* you choose to accept it, is to find the new recruit, Braeden, locate the angel previously known as Edwin, retrieve the stolen Angel Bracelet, recover four stolen dragons from Atlantis, and rescue the Queen Andromeda."

"Karyn, your assignment is to chaperon the group and provide valuable clues, should they get off the beaten path. I have already spoken with Zoltan, and he is prepared to engage one hundred percent."

Karyn responded, "Affirmative, Sir. Anything else I should be aware of?"

Aaron said, "Yes. Karyn?"

"Yes, Sir?" she asked.

"Can you try to be nice to Ashley, at least while you are in her presence? And please, don't throw any more of those metal, circular, Ninja disks at her either. Yes, I know it's just done jokingly and doesn't hurt her."

Aaron laughed at his own comment. The thought of seeing Karyn hitting Ashley, even just for fun, had to make one laugh.

It was a good thing that Ashley was such a good sport. She had just gotten her halo and wings back, so she was not in any mood to get them taken away. Instead, Ashley said, "Oh, don't worry about us. If she gets too annoying I'll just beat her over the head with a dozen roses."

They all laughed at the thought of that. Ashley thought to herself, "*I didn't say which end of the roses I'd hit her with. The thorny side,*" and started laughing.

The four of them all burst out laughing because Ashley had forgotten that they could all hear her thoughts.

What Ashley didn't know was that Karyn was a trained assassin, known for her stealth Ninja techniques. It was very unlikely that anyone would be hitting her with roses, thorns or otherwise. Also, she didn't know that Karyn already had a large file about her that had been used to report things back to the A.C.C. on certain... *events* that she had been involved in. Some things had been good, but most of them had been bad. Oh, *Ashley* didn't kill people, like some of the other demons that Karyn knew, but while she had been on earth, or on any other planet for that matter, she had been the Temptress of Seduction — quite fitting for a Cupid gone rogue.

So while *she* hadn't killed anyone, she had made people kill over her. It was a well-known fact that Ashley had taken form as a mortal in ancient times, causing great wars. Back then, her name had been Helen. Mortals always went to war over three things; power, money, and/or love. Sometimes it was all three, sometimes it was just one.

Technically, Ashley wasn't a "fallen angel". In order to be considered "fallen" she would have had to break an Angel Law, which she hadn't. She just hadn't fulfilled her angelic duty of helping *two* people fall in love with *each other*. Instead, she helped two, or two thousand, all fall in love with *her*. When she was confronted once, she merely stated, "I didn't *make* those married men leave their wives. They chose to go on that crusade. Unfortunately, they fell in love with me."

Aaron finally said, "Now go. Find our little angels and fulfill your duties. Ashley, if you are successful, your reward will be that you get to keep the halo and wings. So, there is a huge incentive for you in there. Karyn, I see a promotion in your near future."

Both of the angels smiled. Ashley said, "I can live with that."

Karyn replied, "Well, you don't have a choice. And for right now, I can live with you. Let's get going, sister."

Together they said, "God love me," and with a flash of bright light and a cloud of Angel Dust, the unlikely duo were gone.

Aaron said out loud, "God help them."

He heard a voice say back, "*I am always helping.*"

23

King of Kings

Aaron tapped his A.B.L. and thought of Zoltan. POOF! With a cloud of dust there he was, looking back at Aaron.

Aaron said, "Greetings, Zoltan. Confirmation. Good luck." He pressed the button and Zoltan was gone.

Jesus grinned and said, "Well, it looks like you have your hands free for now. Do you know who took the dragons?"

Aaron nodded yes and said, "Oh, I already know who it was, where they took them, and why they want them. It was Kylar, a fallen angel from the early 7 B.Y.T. (before your time)."

Jesus nodded and said, "Oh, yes, actually the name *does* ring a bell. Why in heaven would he want a dragon?"

Aaron said, "My best guess is that he wants to take it to another realm to cause havoc and destruction. Before dragons were in Atlantis, they roamed the lands. A magical place called the Enchanted Forest was home to many of them. What concerns me the most is that two of the dragons that were taken are female, and both are expected to lay eggs. We have no idea how when they will lay eggs, or how many, or when they will hatch."

He touched his A.B.L. and thought, "*Kingston,*" and with a puff of gold smoke, a handsome, black-haired angel appeared. He had a short haircut and he looked military-like. He wore a gold headset on his right ear. He also had on yellow-tinted sunglasses, like he was a rifle sharpshooter. Behind those shades were emerald-colored eyes.

"Hello, Kingston, Karyn is on special assignment and I need you to pick up where she left off. As you may have heard, four dragons were stolen from

Atlantis. Two of the females are expected to lay eggs any day now. I have it on God's authority that Kylar was involved, and was last seen in the Yankee Omega galaxy. Yes, I know, directly and straight down as far as you can go, billions of galaxies away."

Kingston flashed a second and then was standing in Aaron's office. He looked over at Jesus and got on one knee. "Greetings, my King; I was unaware you were here."

He wasn't wearing a tunic; instead he looked like he was wearing a white military uniform, and he had black gloves and black boots on.

Jesus smiled and said, "No need to get on one knee. I appreciate the respect." He put his fist out and Kingston gave him a knuckle bump.

Kingston said, "So, after I find the dragons, what am I supposed to do? Capture and retrieve?"

Aaron shook his head no, and instead said, "Oh no, just report the results back to me. We will need to use the information to help Karyn and her band of angels find the dragons. They are going to rescue them. Ever so thankful, Kingston."

Kingston twinkled out and was gone just as quickly as he had appeared.

Aaron looked over at Jesus and said, "He's one of the best. As you know, he was instrumental in the capture of Lucifer."

In the meantime, the band of angels touched down at the Warrior Battle Training Grounds on their distant, home planet of Kieron. It was located just a hop, skip, and a twinkle away from Angel Academy. Angels from all over the universe gathered on Kieron to learn the ways of Warriors. Some angels found that Keiron had been the missing glove that they had been searching for their entire life. Others turned their nose up at the thought of the duties that were required to be a Warrior Angel.

Warriors didn't just defend heaven; they also defended earth and other planets that were facing ultimate destruction. While God gave free will to all of his creatures, the one thing that he *did* safeguard against was their extinction. For example, humans believed that a giant meteor shower rained down on the earth, destroying the dinosaurs, when actually, Warrior Angels were the ones who destroyed the *dinosaurs* in order to prepare the earth for humans. To do so, millions of Warriors and Cupids descended upon earth and lit it up with Light Arrows.

Whenever asteroids get too close to the earth's atmosphere, Warrior Angels appear and shoot them down. From the human eye it would appear that the asteroids had just burned up in the atmosphere.

If angels hadn't defended the skies, and continued to do so, the earth would look like a moon, full of craters. Not only do the Warrior Angels defend the earth against asteroids and meteors, they also protect the earth from alien life forms that continually attempt to attack it.

The planet of Kieron is exactly what one would imagine a training area to be like. It isn't beautiful and lush like many of the other Angel retreats. Instead, it is very military-looking, with gray, concrete walls on the ground. High above it in the skies, thousands of miles above the planet, resides the facility that the angels congregate and reside in. Like Angel Academy, it appears to float magically in the clouds. There are two suns that float and rotate around each other above the planet, and at the bottom are four rotating moons. The planet does not spin, only the suns and moons.

The heart of the planet is covered in giant oceans that go miles below the surface. This is where the deadly mermen from Atlantis train, fight, fence, and slash away in a secret training facility only known to the angels and mermen. Many times, warrior angels practice with the mermen in the underwater lair. There is a secret, magical doorway located a hundred miles under the surface, only known to a few, that leads from Atlantis to Kieron.

In a sudden flash of gold and white light, the five angels twinkled to Kieron, landing just fifty feet above the training headquarters. All four angels, except for Braeden, extended their wings and lit up their halos. This was the first time that Braeden had seen angels make an entrance like this. From the ground, it looked like angels were descending from the heavens with bright lights shining on them. It was quite a spectacle, and any mermen, or other species, that could see their arrival, would be most impressed. He was one of the last ones to float down, and the other four halos were so bright that no one would have noticed that Braeden didn't have a halo or wings. Many of the inhabitants on the planet were shielding their eyes from the bright lights. There weren't any humanoid life forms, but there were thousands of creatures that were native to the planet. Many of earth's extinct species were still alive and well on Kieron.

Zoltan looked around and mentally counted everyone. He said, "All right, we all made it. We are just waiting for two additional angels to join our party."

Braeden looked at Taylor and said, "Who else is joining us? Do you know? Is it another recruit?"

It wasn't even five minutes before a flash of light and a cloud of angel dust appeared above them at fifty feet in the air. Two new angels, with wings extended and halos glowing brightly, came floating down to the surface to the rest of the little group.

Taylor said, "There's your answer. It looks like it's Karyn, from the A.C.C. Special Forces Team, joined by... no, it can't be..." he paused, and didn't finish his sentence.

Braeden looked over and saw that Aleona and Morgan were also in shock in response to who was with them. It was Ashley, the prior Temptress of Seduction, but she didn't look tempting; she looked angelic, and she had on her wings and halo.

Aleona was the first to speak and said, "Holy *mother*... earth!"

Braeden was a little confused and said, "*That* is Mother Earth? I didn't know that Mother Earth looked like an angel."

Ashley laughed and said, "No, cutie, my name is Ashley. I used to be an active Cupid, but I haven't been seen in heaven or the A.C.C. in over five hundred years. Your friends here are a little shocked that I have wings and a halo. But that's okay, they'll get over it. Aaron gave them back to me; Karyn was there. So, *hi!* I am part of your team now." She cleared her throat and said, "Ahem, Jesus said that you guys needed a good sharpshooter, just in case. No offense, Morgan and Zoltan, but we both know who is the best shot around... and it isn't a Warrior or a Trainer."

Braeden exclaimed, "Wow! It's an honor to meet you. I'm Braeden. The last two Cupids that I met were very different. What was it like talking with Jesus?"

Zoltan crossed his arms. Morgan kept silent. Karyn's A.B.L. lit up and she touched it. Aaron's face appeared in a cloud. The cloud said, "Report status."

Karyn looked at him and said, "We have arrived with the team. I will A.B.L. you as soon as I have something to report."

He replied back, "Excellent, ever so thankful," and he blinked out in a cloud of dust.

Ashley said, "It was pretty rad. Jesus always looks different when you see him. The only thing that looks the same are his eyes."

Zoltan interrupted, in his deep voice, and said, "Come now, enough talk. Let us move to the Great Hall. Braeden, you are expected. There is someone there who is very anxious to meet you, and has a *very* special gift for you."

He looked directly at Ashley and said, "Brace yourself for this one, my dear."

Braeden said, "Who is excited to meet me?"

For the first time, Zoltan smiled and said, "Marcia, the Senior Cupid of True Love."

Aaron M. Stephens, M.B.A.

24

Kieron --The Warrior Planet

Aleona and Morgan grinned at each other. Morgan finally said, "Oh *this* is going to be *sooo* good. I would have waited a thousand years just to see Ashley's face when she has to face Marcia." She laughed a sinister laugh.

Braeden didn't like not being in on the secret. *"Will someone please tell me what is so bad that Ashley would hide from Marcia?"*

Ashley thought to him, *"I'll tell you, sweetheart. It's not that big of a deal, really. Well, to some it is. I, 'accidentally' shot an arrow at a couple of people who were not supposed to fall in love with each other; they were both supposed to fall in love with someone else, and as a result those people never got together, and a baby wasn't born or something."*

Braeden looked at her, wondering whom it was that had been shot.

Ashley touched her bracelet to Braeden's and said, *"Did you know there wasn't actually supposed to be a Virgin Mary... but a Virgin Cheri? Heh, heh, heh. Oops. My bad. Paris, not Jerusalem. Do you know how far Paris is from Jerusalem?"* and then she broke the link.

Ashley sashayed, following Zoltan with an innocent smile and said, "One little arrow and you never live it down."

Karyn was following behind the rest of the angels when she floated up next to Braeden, whispering into his ear, "Be careful of her. She has those gloves on for a reason. She pretends to act all innocent, and then you find yourself wanting to like and love her. That's her power." Then she then fell back and floated along with Taylor, Morgan, and Aleona, like they were all longtime best friends.

The seven angels floated their way up to the Great Hall. While the base of the structure was concrete gray, the Great Hall, like Angel Academy, had five white pillars that formed a circle. There were chairs and seating that lined the large, round room, leaving the floor open for guests, speakers, and fighting tournaments. Looking up, there were additional seats for thousands more. Unlike other places that Braeden had visited, this one had floating fire torches all around, filling the arena with light.

In one of the large throne chairs sat Marcia, along with Drake and Illana on either side. Zoltan positioned himself in one of the chairs on the opposite side of the room from Marcia. Morgan, Taylor, Aleona, and Karyn all took the remaining chairs beside Zoltan, leaving Braeden and Ashley standing in the middle of the room by themselves.

Marcia sat high on her throne, and she held a golden scepter in her right hand. At the top of it were ornate wings with a red ruby heart at the very tip that sparkled and shined. Marcia's long, golden hair was now a white color, and was done up in a very elegant, braided hairdo. She wasn't wearing earrings and she no longer had on the diamond bracelet with a red ruby heart. Braeden could only assume that it was perched on top of her scepter. She wore a simple, yet elegant, long, flowing gown with the same braided edging that Braeden's tunic had. He could see gold high-heeled shoes underneath her dress. Her halo shone brightly as if a spotlight was directly over her.

The Great Hall was silent.

Marcia finally spoke and said, "Hello, little Braeden. I have been waiting for you." She smiled and he felt good. She looked directly at Ashley and said, "And Ashley, if this isn't *my* lucky day. I haven't seen you... in over two thousand years? With wings *and* a halo? Somebody has been extra good to get those back." She was cold, and narrowed her eyes at Ashley.

There was a sudden chill in the room. The Great Hall went completely dark, and then a bright gold ball of light appeared in the center of the room, directly above Ashley and Braeden.

The chill was gone. Instead, a warm feeling filled everyone in the room.

The same P.A. voice, loud, clear, deep baritone, stated, "*All is forgiven. There will be no punishment, only love for these two. I have spoken.*"

The ball of light vanished and everyone was silent.

Zoltan finally broke the silence and said, "And so it

is. Marcia, I believe you have something for Braeden. Ashley, you may be seated."

Ashley looked, and there was an empty seat next to Zoltan. She floated over to it and quietly sat down.

The lights came back on and the torches were burning bright again. Marcia floated down from her chair, and was floating just above Braeden. She leaned down and kissed him on the forehead just like she had done to the baby Jesus. He felt a tingle. She smiled, and then finally said, "My little Braeden, you have been given the gift of Love in the form of your first Angel Bow. Simply think of a traditional bow or a crossbow."

His angel bracelet lit up and a very tiny, little, red ruby heart was embedded into the inside of it. She floated back up to her throne chair.

Next, Zoltan was up. The lights focused on him and in his deep, baritone voice, he said, "An angel is no Warrior without the proper tools."

He floated down from his chair and touched Braeden's forehead with his index finger. Braeden's bracelet magically became an inch thicker, and now bore the angelic insignia symbol that matched Zoltan's tattoo.

"Think of a sword and it will appear. Fight with love and it will burst with flames. Think of a shield and it will extract from your bracelet."

Braeden stood there for a moment and thought, first of a bow, and a small gold bow appeared in his right hand. He let go of the thought and it shrank to a small ball and dissolved. He imagined a sword. A small white knife appeared. Everyone chuckled.

Zoltan said, "It will take some practice, but you will get the hang of it."

Braeden said, "Thank you. I am ever most grateful. Can you tell me why I would want to be a Cupid or a Warrior?"

Marcia said, "Of course, I would be delighted to tell you!"

She waved her staff in the air and a chair appeared for Braeden to sit on. Like in Atlantis, he was prepared for a really cool story. Learning about a Cupid was something he never really gave much thought or attention to while on earth. He honestly thought that they were like fairies — something pretend and made up for kids. After all, he couldn't remember ever falling in love as a human.

Marcia smiled and said, "Just because you don't remember your true love now, doesn't mean you didn't have one, or that you don't have one. I happen to know for a fact that there was someone on earth who loved you very much."

25

Fight! Fight! Fight!

Braeden blinked, silently thinking to himself, "*Me? I had a true love? Can it really be? I don't remember, and don't feel anything for anyone.*"

Marcia said, "That is because in order for you to be an angel, all evidence of past or former encounters had to be removed so that you could serve the Lord. In the past, some angels thought they could... cheat the system."

She looked directly at Ashley and said, "We know that there are loopholes in the system. We know that this is not a perfect system. We strive to follow God's orders so it is the best that it can be. One thing is for certain, and that is that there is not enough love to go around, hence the reason that a *good* Cupid, a sharp shooter on the bow, is a valuable member of the team."

Braeden raised his hand and Marcia let him speak. "Can you tell me why I never heard anything about a Cupid as a human? What exactly does a Cupid do? Are there requirements as to how many people have to fall in love?"

Marcia looked over at Drake ,and the lights turned onto him. He looked devastatingly handsome, and Braeden wondered, if *he* became a Cupid, would he be handsome too?

Drake smiled, showing his perfect white teeth. He said to Braeden, "Yes, Braeden, you would become even *more* handsome than you are now, should you decide to be a Cupid. Cupids were not always this way. Over time, our role has evolved as the universe has evolved. Many eons ago we were used as fighters, many times to attack and defend. We were rarely on earth. It has only been within the past few thousand years that we have occupied earth. In order to be a Cupid, you must first train here at the Warrior Training Grounds to learn mastery over your sword *and* your bow, and then can you apply to be a Cupid. Once you are accepted as a Cupid you will have to attempt to get two mortals to fall in love. Sometimes we are successful, sometimes... eh, well, let's just say it isn't meant to be. Being a Cupid isn't just shooting a bow and then on to the next person. No, you have to infiltrate both of those people, act as their friend, and help get them together. Words of encouragement and support are really a Cupid's powers."

Braeden was under the impression that if he wanted to be a Cupid, he could just be a Cupid. Not that he had to train and apply. What was up with that?

Drake continued, "Yes, it is true that we need Cupids. We need trustworthy, dependable Cupids who follow orders. Just like in the normal prayer chain of command, prayers for love are also answered, and Cupids are dispatched from one assignment to another. Our lives are very different from other angels, as we actually live on earth among humans."

It was beginning to make sense to Braeden. He wasn't sure what he wanted to do yet... he hadn't known that it was a lengthy process. What if he couldn't make up his mind? What would happen to him then?

Zoltan spoke in his deep, baritone voice and said, "Those are all good questions, and if you don't find an occupation, one will be found *for* you. Such as, something manual, like Angel Dust clean up crew. How would you like to go around cleaning up dust?"

Braeden said, "I have never seen anyone cleaning up Angel Dust. I think you are teasing me."

Zoltan snapped his fingers and a cloud of dust fell to the floor. Everyone watched it. Braeden hadn't really paid much attention to what happened to all the Angel Dust, he figured it just magically disappeared on its own. The dust landed on the floor and Zoltan waved his right hand in a circular motion. Three tiny, little angels, half his size and previously invisible, magically appeared. Sure enough, they were sweeping up the dust and putting it in little containers. When they were done, they disappeared instead of twinkled. There was a flash of light, but no dust left behind.

"You see? I'm not teasing you, Braeden. You could end up working in the A.C.C., however, that is not a job I would recommend. Some of the leadership there," he looked at Karyn, "can be a little... eh... challenging at times. No freedom at all. Chained to your headset." Zoltan crossed his arms.

Braeden stood there for a moment, thinking of different weapons; bows, swords... making them appear and vanish into dust. He stopped for a moment and thought of all the clean up crew he was making work for, and he stopped. Yes, he was certain that he did not want to be cleaning up dust after other angels. The only up side was that he would be able to travel the universe... no harm, no assets, no worries. How hard could it be to train as a Warrior and then as a sharp shooter? He sort of liked the idea of going back to earth as a Cupid. The only thing better than that was to get promoted to "Earth Angel." Earth Angels can actually *hear* other angels, because they *are* angels in human form.

Braeden looked up at Marcia and said, "How do I become an Earth Angel?"

She said, "Simple. You have to be promoted after being a Cupid."

Zoltan spoke, "Oh, we aren't going to throw you to the wolves just yet. That wouldn't be very nice, would it?"

Zoltan floated down from his throne chair and touched two fingers to Braeden's forehead. Suddenly, Braeden was filled with experiences, knowledge, wisdom, and memories from millions of other Warrior Angels.

"Accept this as another gift, the collective consciousness and wisdom of all the Warriors. It will greatly enhance your skills."

Braeden looked down at his wrist and again thought of a sword. This time, instead of a little, white, shark knife, he manifested a glowing sword, seven feet long, and it was burning with white fire. He swung it around his body, making an invisible figure eight.

Zoltan said, "Excellent! Most impressive, young Braeden. Now... time for you to use some of that skill on your first test."

He pressed a button on his A.B.L. and the floor began to shift and open. Braeden jumped and began to float in order to avoid falling through. Down below were monsters so fierce that he began to shudder. An invisible force shield went up between the observers and what would soon be a fight below. Braeden looked and saw that there were two ways out; up and down, and he didn't like what he saw below him. Two harpies, to be exact. Each was carrying a black sword about three feet long. Braeden's sword was twice that size, so he should have no problem at all, right?

The floor continued to drop even further, and what he saw below that was even scarier. Were they kidding?

He looked over at Zoltan and shouted, "Really? Is this for real? You are going to make me fight two harpies and a *dragon?!*"

"Yes!" he shouted back, "And you are going to do just fine. Just remember what I taught you. They can't kill you, but they *can* hurt and wound you."

"Oh, just wonderful. I can't die but they can hurt me. Oh, this is going to be just so much fun."

Actually, it *was* kind of fun. For the first time, he flew around fending off a black sword at every turn. He was ever so thankful that Zoltan had touched his forehead. Now he was fighting like a real Warrior, not just some kid pretending to be something he wasn't, like in a Nintendo video game.

All of the sudden, something new and exciting happened to Braeden. He wasn't just a lone Warrior fighting two ugly winged women with swords. Now Braeden could see into the future.

26

Eww. Dragon Breath.

This was incredible. Braeden had never been able to see into the future, probably because he didn't have a need to. Now he was up against two really ugly women with large, black wings and sharp talons, and each was swinging a sword at him. Fortunately, he was faster than they were, and he was always one step ahead of them. So, this seeing into the future, that was how angels always had the upper-hand advantage.

With this new power it was almost like he was watching a show in fast forward. He knew what they were going to do before they did it. He spun around quickly, surprising one of the harpies. He stabbed his white sword behind him, right through the heart of one harpie. She exploded into black dust. The other one was furious! She caught her sister's black sword and came tearing out of the black pit with rage and fury.

Braeden grabbed his gold bow, and he manifested an arrow by thinking of it. It was black. That was okay. He pulled the string on the bow as far back as it could go. He let it go, and it sailed through the air before hitting her in the right wing. She flinched, but it didn't stop her. *Silver Arrow.* POOF. He let it fly and it hit her in the leg. She screamed in pain. *Whatever the silver arrow did, it was good.* He looked down and the dragon was starting to rouse. It breathed fire all over the arena. He could feel the heat rising from so much fire, but oddly enough, it didn't hurt him. The harpie, on the other hand, was hurting big time. Whatever those arrows did, it seemed to cause her great suffering. The dragon moved a few feet and Braeden could see why it wasn't attacking... yet. It had two huge chains around its front and back legs. It couldn't move until Zoltan gave the word. For now, all it could do was blow fire at Braeden, and at the remaining harpie.

Suddenly he could hear Zoltan, Enyah, and Marcia talking in his head. *"All you have to do is think of what you want and it will magically appear out of Angel Dust."* He knew exactly what he needed to do to beat this harpie. He looked at her feet, still carrying both of the black swords in each claw. He pictured her claws and then imagined two gigantic, heavy ball and chains weighing her down. Instantly, a cloud of gold dust appeared around her claws, clamping down, forcing her to drop the blades and use all of her might to stay flying in the air. It was no use; the more she tried, the bigger Braeden imagined the heavy ball and chain.

She had no way to release the chains, and she no longer had her swords as they had fallen harmlessly next to the now angry, fire-breathing dragon. She screamed and squawked, trying to get loose. The large balls fell toward the ground with such weight and force that when they crashed down on the dragon it screamed in pain. Braeden had managed to position the harpie so that each large weight landed on either side of the dragon, forcing its head to lie on the ground, defenseless and vulnerable. The dragon was so angry that it breathed fire for the longest five minutes of Braeden's life. The harpie, pinned to the ground, screamed as the flames burned her to a crisp. She was reduced to a pile of black ashes.

Zoltan unlocked the dragon's feet, but it was no use. The two large balls connected to a chain, and had the dragon trapped. Braeden floated down next to the dragon, just out of harms way. The dragon had used up all of its energy and could not even blow a smoke puff if it wanted to. There was no way it was going to free itself from the heavy weights that forced its head to the ground. The dragon knew it was over. All Braeden had to do was take one swift chop and it would be dead. The dragon closed its eyes and a tear dropped from its eyes.

Then Braeden heard, "*Please, don't kill me. I did nothing to you but save you from a harpie. I am innocent. I am just a little boy. I was hatched a few days ago. Where is my mommy? I am all alone. I am afraid. Please. Please. Please.*"

Braeden thought back to him, "*Hey, little fellow, it's okay. I'm Braeden. What's your name?*"

The dragon answered back, "*They called me Orrin.*"

Braeden thought back, "*Do you know who did this to you? Who brought you here?*"

Orrin said, in his mind, "*A week before I hatched I was aware of my surroundings. I was still in my shell and I could vaguely see two people through the shell. I could hear voices, but not thoughts like I can now. I was sold to the people who brought me here.*"

Like Braeden, this innocent creature was new to the world; he was defenseless, and also like Braeden, had no wings. Braeden couldn't kill an innocent, little, baby dragon. Sure, he was already over one hundred feet tall, and could easily wreak havoc and destruction, but something inside Braeden said, "*No, I will not let you die by my hand for sport or training.*"

Instead, he thought, "*I love you, little dragon Orrin. I will not harm you. Instead, I will take you somewhere where you will always be safe and you will never have to fight for your life.*" He reached down and touched the dragon's forehead, and said, "I love you. God love us."

There was a flash of bright light and a cloud of Angel Dust, and the two were gone. The arena was silent.

Zoltan finally broke the silence. "What did he just do? WHERE DID HE GO?"

Morgan looked down at her A.B.L. as if she

were reading a book or deciphering a message. She finally said, "There. I sense him now. He thinks he is pretty cool since he can twinkle on his own. What he doesn't know is that I am always attached to him. He's heading toward Atlantis."

Karyn had already seen what was going on, and long before Braeden twinkled out of there she had already gone back to the A.C.C. to report what had just happened back to Aaron. No one even noticed she was gone.

"ATLANTIS!" everyone said at once.

Zoltan grinned and said, "You really have to admire this one. He may earn his wings and a halo today, but he will *never* be a Warrior!"

27

Grow a Pair ... of Wings

Braeden had never twinkled another living creature before, so he wasn't sure he was even doing it right. It was only a matter of minutes before he arrived in Atlantis. He and Orrin sparkled and exploded in a burst of gold light and glitter. Like the other angels, he was fifty feet up in the sky when he arrived. For the first time in his existence, he had a shining halo *and* what appeared to be a small set of junior wings. Braeden hadn't even noticed his halo until Orrin thought to him, "*Nice wings and halo. They look good on you. Thank you for saving my life.*"

Braeden did it. He saved a life. He did a good deed,

and now his wings were starting to grow, and a little, softly glowing halo shined on his entire body, lighting up the ground below him. Yes indeed, it was a good feeling and a good day. So this was what saving a life felt like. This certainly was the best day of his life... as an angel. He was pretty sure that he had never saved a life as a human; that takes courage, strength, and bravery. He was brave. It was not easy standing up to a dragon.

Orrin looked over at Braeden and thought, "*I will never forget it. I owe you my life, and a life debt.*"

Braeden was beaming with happiness and literally glowing. He said, "Oh no! What if I get in trouble for saving you? What is going to happen to me now? Am I going to get in trouble for saving a dragon?" He started to get worried for the first time as an angel. He heard a soft female voice behind him and he turned.

"Hello, Braeden. You are not in trouble, and in fact it is just the opposite. As you may now have noticed, you have grown your first pair of wings. As you *also* may have noticed, there is a feeling associated with every good deed that you do. Saving a life is a very high priority and it is rewarded. Thank you for saving this little baby dragon. As you may know, his mother, father, aunt, and uncle were all kidnapped a short while ago." There stood Desiree, a very beautiful, young, sophisticated-looking Senior Angel.

Like all of the other Seniors, Desiree wore an identical name tag, matching bracelet, and a silver tunic with braided edging. Her tunic was slightly different in that it was longer, like a dress, and just barely touched the ground. Her dark, red hair was in a very intricate French braid. It was very long, and Braeden imagined that it was even longer than Queen Andromeda's if she let it down. She did not have her wings or halo turned on.

She said to Braeden, "Congratulations on your wings and halo. You are, of course, welcome to leave them on for as long as you like."

She smiled and turned, and started walking toward the palace. Orrin, who was sitting patiently, got up and started to walk alongside Desiree. Braeden ran to catch up with her.

Reaching Desiree he said, "Desiree, can you tell me something?"

"Of course, what would you like to know?"

"Was I supposed to kill this dragon as part of my training? Or was I supposed to save him?"

She stopped, looked at him, and said, "Well, those are very nice wings and a beautiful new halo. Do you think God would have rewarded you with wings and a halo if you had destroyed something so young and innocent?"

He said, "I... I... don't know. I was told to always obey God, or else."

Desiree said, "And did God tell you to kill two harpies and a baby dragon?"

He looked at her and then down at the ground, and said, "No, Ma'am. He didn't. Zoltan did."

"Is *Zoltan*... God?" she continued.

"No, Ma'am, he isn't," he replied quietly.

Desiree said, "Then I think you did the right thing. Come along now, there are some folks here that have heard what you have done and are really excited to meet you. Word travels fast on Angel Radio. I have a team of angels who are currently investigating our missing dragons, as well as a team searching for the

Queen. It's all very upsetting that we've had a break-in."

Desiree touched her A.B.L. and thought of Kaili. Instantly, a cloud of dust appeared, and a beautiful little angel with long, white hair in a ponytail appeared. She looked like a little girl.

"Kaili, Braeden has rescued one of the baby dragons. This one is named Orrin. Can you come take him to his new home, please?"

She appeared in a poof of gold dust, and had what looked like a really big, gold leash for Orrin. Kaili was just adorable. It was hard to believe that this little girl was going to wrangle a dragon into following her.

Braeden said, "She is seriously going to put that on him and he's going to let her?"

"Why not?" said Kaili, "He knows it is so he won't fall behind or get lost. It's for his own protection. Just like he likes you, he likes me, too. It's part of my charm." She grinned her pearly white teeth, and sure enough, when she held out the leash, Orrin leaned down so that she could put it around his neck.

Orrin looked over at Braeden and thought, "*It's true, boss. I can hear her thoughts just like I can hear yours.*"

The gold, glowing leash magically got bigger and longer. Kaili jumped into the air and her wings exploded on her back. She floated alongside Orrin. He didn't have any wings yet, but he didn't need them. He was so big that she needed to fly to keep up with him.

As they were trotting off, Orrin turned his giant head, looked back at Braeden, and said, "*If you ever need me for anything, just call out my name three times in your head and I will hear you. I will come to help you whenever or wherever.*"

Braeden didn't know it, but Orrin was already talking in his head to his family that was still in Atlantis. Braeden thought back to him, "*But how will you find me if you are in Atlantis? You can't leave, you know.*"

Orrin said, "*We dragons have secrets too. While you were talking with Desiree, I was talking with my family, and I know some things you don't. Thanks again, Boss, I'll be seeing you in the next hundred years or so.*"

Braeden wasn't sure what that meant but he wasn't too concerned. He had done his good deed, and he needed to get back to his friends. After talking with Desiree he was certain he had done the right thing. After all, he *did* have wings now. He turned and made them flap, just for fun. Angel Dust fell to the ground.

He turned to Desiree and said, "Desiree, would it be okay if I spread my wings and flew around Atlantis for a little bit?"

Just as she was about to answer, there was a flash of light and gold glitter dust and there, floating above them fifty feet up, was Aleona, as beautiful as ever. As an Angel of Light, her entrance was beyond spectacular. Braeden and Desiree were hypnotized by its radiance. Unlike the last few times he had seen her, she was dressed in battle gear with large, metal shields over her wings, called Wing Guards, to protect them from damage. They made her look fierce.

"There you are, my friend! We were starting to get worried about you. We thought you got lost," Aleona said with a grin. "I also wanted to spend some alone time with you, Braeden. After all, shouldn't you learn what an Angel of Light actually *does*?"

She noticed Braeden looking at her wing guards. She retracted her wings and the guards instantly turned to dust. "I just wear those when I don't know what I am flying into. They tend to get a reaction from those watching from below. Sasha designed them. They have other cool features too, like that they make my wings incredibly strong and invincible against arrows."

He had to admit that Aleona, like Morgan when she was all white-eyed, looked pretty scary at first. He said to her, "I was just about to spread my wings for the first time and fly around Atlantis for a little bit. Any chance you'd like to join me for a spin?"

She had been to Atlantis many times. She knew how big it really was and that there were a great number of things that could easily distract a brand new, little angel. After thinking about it, she thought of something else that might be more exciting. She said, "Hey, I have a great idea! Let's fly back to Kieron and we can go 'Angel of Light' style. How does that sound?"

Braeden wasn't sold on that idea, however he *did* like the idea of exploring a magical land that disappeared from humanity long before he was even born. Aleona knew that she was going to lose really fast unless she did something extreme.

"Hey, I have another idea... we can ride a comet there, and you can have Zoltan take you to Purgatory."

Now she was talking. Ride a comet? Heavens, *yes!* He said, "Wow, and how exactly are you going to get a comet to come by here and fly us all the way to Kieron?"

"Easy," she said, "Who do you think *makes* comets anyway? Angels of Light make comets."

28

Angel of Light

Had Braeden heard Aleona correctly? Ride a comet back to Kieron? Seriously? Was she for real?

Aleona smiled and said, "Yes, I am for real," and she poked him in the chest.

Braeden looked over at Desiree and said, "I promise I will come back and visit another time! Take care of Orrin for me. For some reason I really feel attached to him."

Aleona said, "You're not an Angel of Light so you don't have this special power, but if you choose so, you can. An Angel of Light is called upon in the darkest of times. When man has lost all hope and there is nothing left but a prayer, I am called upon. I bring forward hope, goodness, strength, vitality, and most of all... faith."

She closed her eyes and unfolded her wings and halo. Her wings kept getting bigger and bigger until all Braeden could see was white light. He reached out for her and she touched his hands. He felt what she had been talking about. He could feel all those emotions welling up inside of him, and it made him feel good. He never wanted to let go of her hand.

He wondered when she was going to make a comet? He had always wanted to see one when he was a mortal, but it never quite happened. He looked over and thought, "I'm ready when you are. To make the comet and ride it, that is."

She smiled and said, "Braeden, look down and around. We are the comet. We have been flying through galaxies for over a year now. We should reach Kieron within the next five years. Enjoy it while it lasts."

They blasted through a helix nebula and a cat's eye nebula. It was pretty amazing. He thought, "I wish I had my iPod with me. I feel like I should be in a movie hearing a cool soundtrack."

She laughed and snapped her finger. A cloud of gold dust appeared, and suddenly there was an iPod in her hand. She said, "*I have mine, wanna hear my favorite playlist?*"

How could he resist an offer like that?

She said, "There was a song that originally came from the Garden of Angels, I'm not sure which muse it was that hummed it, but later it was put in a movie. I felt like it was written for *me* since I am always riding a comet, or as some people say, riding a star."

She pressed a couple of buttons and "Rule the World" by Gary Barlow started to play. "We ride in style, my friend." When they got to the line in the song that said, "We can ride on a star," she squeezed his hand and said, "See why this is my song?"

They flew in silence, listening to the song and watching all the magnificent wonders of the universe. Braeden had no idea where they were. Then the comet shot upwards, and began picking up speed. He looked up and saw a black hole.

He looked over at Aleona. She thought to him, "*You got it, we are going through there.*"

He wasn't sure what was going to happen. He waited

a moment, and then... nothing. They popped out of the other side as if it wasn't even there. They started to slow down, and in the distance he could see the planet of Kieron with its two suns on the top of the planet and the four moons on the bottom. Seeing the suns and moon rotate around a stationary planet was amazing.

As soon as they were a few hundred kilometers from the planet, Aleona went even slower. Her light started to retract and slowly fade out until she and Braeden were just a faint glow. She put her hand out and stopped Braeden.

"Wait, something isn't right," she said.

"Whatever do you mean?" asked Braeden.

"As an Angel of Light I can hear things you can't hear, and right now what I *can't* hear are the conversations and thoughts of thousands of Warrior Angels," she said, deep in thought.

What could have happened since she had been gone? They floated down to the planet. It was quiet and the busy activity that Braeden had seen earlier was nowhere to be seen. They made their way to the Great Hall where Braeden had been earlier. The torches were blown out and the seats were all empty.

Braeden said, "Where do you think everyone went? Is this normal?"

Aleona responded, "No, this is highly unusual. I think we've seen enough. We should get back to the A.C.C. to see what is going on."

She touched her A.B.L. and thought of Morgan. A flash of dust and then there was nothing... no Morgan, no bright lights. Something was definitely not right.

Aleona did not like the way things were looking and sounding. Not being able to reach Morgan on the A.B.L. was not normal. She looked at Braeden and said, "Let's go," and the two of them twinkled in a flash of light and dust.

"God love me," they said, and they were gone.

29

Daddy's Favorite Little Angel

Zoltan was furious. Never, in all of his time as a Senior Angel, had a new recruit been clever enough to pin down the dragon! Why, that was like cheating! He was supposed to try to *slay* the dragon, or at least shoot it down with some of his harmless angel arrows. Braeden hadn't known that his arrows couldn't hurt a dragon, and he'd had a flaming sword... Zoltan thought for sure that Braeden would have sliced through the dragon's neck and cut off his head. But no, he never took that chance. He'd never taken the life of another creature before, and he wasn't going to, at least not this year.

What little Braeden didn't know, is that dragon armor acts as the strongest shield in the world. The reason these dragons were feared so much was because even angels have difficulty penetrating the armor. Dragons have to be coaxed and convinced with love. Dragons possess a certain kind of magic that protects them. Each magical creature has their own individual ability that makes them special and unique. For example, a fully-grown unicorn has the ability to teleport from one galaxy to another, but not across the universe. It's not as effective as twinkling is for angels, but for the unicorn it works great as a defense mechanism. Even angels can only twinkle partial distances.

Recruits were supposed to fight like there was no tomorrow, and then, when they realized that they couldn't win, Zoltan would go in and save the day, proving what a *real* Warrior could do. But nope, it didn't quite work out that way. The whole thing was a setup from the beginning. The battle was planned out in order to see how well Braeden would do against unbelievable odds. Three to one wasn't really fair. But then again, Zoltan wasn't really fair. Zoltan would argue that he never told Braeden anything. He'd say that he just put up the shield so that Braeden couldn't get out in a conventional way. It's true that he never once commanded, "Kill that harpie. Destroy that dragon."

The invisible shield went down, and Marcia finally spoke.

"Well, Zoltan, it looks like your plan backfired, didn't it? I think this one has a lot of love in his heart. I am pretty sure Orrin was speaking to Braeden in his mind, and convinced him not to kill him."

Zoltan shouted, "THAT'S NOT HOW IT WORKS! He was supposed to attempt to slay the dragon, and when his sword struck the dragon's neck he would be accepted into the Warrior Command!"

Marcia laughed and said, "Who would have thought to use two balls and a chain to pin down a dragon? I think he's rather clever. Well, it looks like my work here is done. Come along, my sweethearts." She snapped her finger and twinkled in flash of light and a swirling cloud of dust. Illana and Drake were right behind her.

"That's not FAIR! Who taught him how to twinkle? Morgan! It was YOU, wasn't it?!" shouted Zoltan.

She flipper her chestnut hair over her bare shoulder

and smirked. She said, "Well... I would like to take credit as his mentor, but alas, it was not me. He wasn't supposed to know how to do that... yet."

Zoltan screamed, "I WANT ANSWERS AND I WANT THEM NOW!" The torches flared up ten feet high with his rage and screaming.

The room went dark and all the torches blew out again.

Everyone was silent.

A small, gold ball of light appeared in the center of the Great Hall, illuminating everyone in the room. The ball floated over to Zoltan and then got very bright. It was so bright that everyone who was left in the room had to shield their eyes.

The ball of gold light finally spoke and it said, "*I taught him how to do that. I have spoken.*" The ball got bigger and bigger until the entire room was filled with light.

Zoltan got down on one knee. No one could see him because it was so bright. He said, "Apologies, my King. I did not know Thee had given him twinkling power. Forgive my rudeness."

The ball of light then said, "*Forgiven. Zoltan, please report to the A.C.C.. Aaron has a special assignment for the Warriors.*"

The room flashed and exploded in light and dust, and then was back to normal again.

Morgan and Taylor looked at each other. Wow, that wasn't something that happened very often. God never interferes or shows up twice on the planet of Kieron in one day. Well, not that anyone knew of anyway.

Morgan thought, "*I wonder what is going on. I am sure we are going to find out really soon.*" She then said, out loud, "Zoltan, what about Braeden? You are supposed to take him on a ride to Purgatory. Shouldn't someone go get him and find out what he did with that dragon?"

Zoltan glared at Morgan and said, "Hello? Seriously? I have to go report to Aaron. Braeden is just going to have to wait to go to Purgatory. Can't you tell that the universe is falling apart again, and I have to go save the day?"

Taylor and Karyn seemed to agree. Braeden had been gone for quite some time. Ashley, new to the party, kept quiet. She liked the attention on someone else for a change.

Aleona finally spoke up, "Fine. I will go get him and bring him back." She exploded in a poof of dust.

Zoltan didn't say anything but touched his A.B.L., and he, too, was gone.

The angels remaining were the most unlikely foursome imaginable. Taylor, and three beautiful angels. One dark-haired, Ashley, one black-haired, Karyn, and one light brunette-haired angel, Morgan.

Taylor said, "Well, that leaves just the four of us. I feel like I should be sending you on a special mission, and my name should actually be *Charlie*".

They all laughed and Morgan said, "One of us needs to be a blond." She snapped her finger and a cloud of dust swirled around her. Then she had new, long, blond hair, worn in a ponytail.

Taylor wasn't kidding about the mission. There were still four dragons loose and a missing Queen, her Herald, and a Cracken. Braeden held a very important clue that the team would need in order to venture onto their next task.

Taylor's A.B.L. lit up, and a small cloud of dust appeared with Rachel's lovely face smiling through at them.

"Taylor, I have located the *file* you were seeking and it has been... ahem,... escorted to a different destination. Also, on other," she looked around as if someone were watching her or listening, "business... it appears that, in another part of the galaxy, an inorganic life form is causing utter destruction, and that Aaron will be sending the Warrior Command to deal with it."

He nodded and said, "Ever so thankful, Rachel. That is all." She poofed out in a cloud of dust.

Ashley looked very confused at this point.

Morgan finally blurted it out, "Well, we might as well tell you. You are going to find out eventually. We were secretly spying on Edwin, because we saw him being taken out of Suzanne's office by two Warrior Angels, along with Drake, Illana, *and* Marcia. Edwin has done something really bad and lost his wings, and he and his powers have been bound by his halo. We are going to rescue him before he is..." she stopped, not wanting to say the rest of it.

"Terminated?" said Ashley. She didn't know that actual angels could die. She had always thought they, like God, were immortal.

"Oh, no! They aren't going to terminate him. An angel can't ever die," said Taylor, "an angel, however, *can* be turned into something else so that they aren't an angel anymore, in a sense making them mortal. I know for a fact that Ivana, a fallen angel from back in the 5000 B.C., was found stealing mortal hearts, and was turned into a water fairy. I am pretty sure she is still off in a place called 'Oz'."

Ashley snorted, "A water fairy? Are you fluffing with me?"

Taylor floated over to Ashley, flew up in her face, and said, "You think I'd ruffle *your* feathers? Ha! That will be the day!"

Morgan snapped back with a cold stare, "NO, we're not ruffling your feathers. I wouldn't touch you to scratch you. This is serious, and if you are going to be a part of this team, you are going to have to remember who is who around here!"

Ashley exclaimed, "You're no higher than I am. You aren't one of Daddy's favorites anymore. I am. Why else would he show up to defend me in front of Marcia?"

Morgan coolly said, "You can get off your little cloud missy, I don't see a number nine anywhere. Taylor is still acting Leader. *He* is the only Senior Angel around here that I see, and although we aren't in his domain, he still outranks both of us. So, you got your wings and halo back. Big deal. It doesn't really prove anything. Daddy forgives everyone. Marcia and I, on the other wing, well, that's another story. Are you with us or not?"

30

Seriously. The world is going to end.

Ashley looked over at Karyn, and quickly remembered the agreement with Aaron and Jesus. She sighed heavily, and said, "Well, I am certainly not against you. Let's get this show on the road."

Karyn spoke up and said, "*Our* mission is to retrieve and rescue. I have it on higher authority that we need to proceed to the Yankee Omega quadrant. We need to go to the planet Aldea, which is close to a lifeless planet called Cybertron. Sources show that the missing A.B.L., stolen centuries ago, is being weaponized, and that somehow, inorganic mechanical robot creatures are coming to life."

Taylor exclaimed, "Aldea! Of course! It is an entire planet hidden by a cloaking device. We recorded it in the system as being mythical, in order to thwart enemies. It looks like this is going to be a divided team for now. Morgan and I will go to Aldea and the two of you go to Cybertron. Report back to the A.C.C. as soon as you uncover any suspicious activity, or the dragons."

Karyn looked over at Ashley, with a sneer, and snapped her fingers. All of the sudden her cute little outfit became a Ninja assault uniform with two long Ninja swords, one for each hand. A scarf covered her mouth and she put on a white eye-mask, like Zoltan's. She looked deadly.

Ashley, not wanting to be outdone, snapped her fingers and was instantly back in a combat outfit. It was nothing like Karyn's... Ashley was back in her long, flowing, see-through cape, and she had gold arm bands on each wrist. She also wore decorative arm bands on her biceps. She carried a long sword and wore a long, flowing, white dress.

Ashley looked over at Karyn and smirked. "You know, it's not like anyone can actually see or hurt you," said Ashley.

Karyn ignored her. She had chosen her stealth-mode attire so that other angels couldn't see her. She thought Ashley was a waste of her time, but she wasn't going to start a fight. There was a promotion to be earned, and she wanted it badly.

Karyn said, "Let's do this." She reached over and grabbed Ashley's hand. "I know where we are going. To CYBERTRON!" There was a flash of light and a cloud of dust, and Taylor and Morgan were left alone.

Morgan looked over at Taylor and said, "ALDEA," and then she and Taylor were nothing but a pile of dust.

Meanwhile, back at the command center, Zoltan blinked and flashed, and he was standing outside the door of Aaron's office. He wasn't too thrilled about God ordering him into Aaron's office, but he knew the rules. *Always obey God.* Or else.

It was the "or else" that scared him the most. As the Senior, he was well aware of what happened to bad angels, and what became of them. He remembered Daxter. Daxter was an obnoxious Herald that was always showing off and talking back. He was sentenced to live five lifetimes on earth as a shelter animal. It only takes one lifetime of animal trans-formation for an angel to learn really quickly. No, if God was ordering him into the A.C.C. then it was for official business, probably because of a world that was facing extinction. They had been too late when the planet of Romulus exploded because of a super-nova. Yes, that had been an unfortunate day, indeed.

He stood there, waiting patiently. Aaron was busy talking with other angels, and Zoltan could see that he was seventh in line to speak with him. Whatever was going on, it was something super-important. He glanced around the A.C.C., and as always, it looked like chaos was going on in one world or another. Aaron finally motioned for Zoltan to come in.

Zoltan stood there silently, awaiting orders.

"Greetings, Zoltan, ever so thankful to see you. I am afraid that the training with Braeden is going to be put temporarily on hold. There is utter chaos and planetary destruction about to happen, and I need all Warrior Angels dispatched immediately," said Aaron.

"Where are we going? And whom are we saving?" asked Zoltan.

"There is a planetary system in the Zeus galaxy that is at risk. It has a peaceful colony of about 1.5 billion inhabitants. The Warrior Command must save this planet and all of its natives. You are going to need all of your Warriors for this mission. I cannot dispatch any other assistance as there are troubles in other sectors of the universe."

Zoltan inquired, "Can you at least tell me what it is that we are up against? Is it alive? Supernatural? An asteroid belt that is going to pulverize the planet?"

Aaron said, with a very serious look on his face, "A star has somehow entered into a black hole's gravitational force, and is now on track to collide with the planet. You are going to be up against a Super Giant category star, the largest star in the universe, usually measuring over 860 million miles across in diameter. You only have three years before the planet, and all its inhabitants, will be completely annihilated."

Zoltan touched his A.B.L. and a miniature map appeared, showing a small galaxy with about one hundred smaller planets. The Super Giant looked like it was a long way away, and made the planets look like tiny, little dots.

"This is unbelievable, there is no way we can save all

those little systems at once!" exclaimed Zoltan. "Any suggestions on a plan of action, Sir?"

Aaron said, "Of course I have a plan of action. You, and your Warrior Command, are going to twinkle that star from its current course trajectory, and send it somewhere else. I am uploading the coordinates to your A.B.L. now. You now have two and a half years, I would suggest you get a move on."

Zoltan nodded and said, "Aye aye, Sir!" He touched his A.B.L. and he was gone in a flash of light.

Braeden and Aleona flashed, and with a cloud of gold glitter dust they were standing in the entryway of the A.C.C.. Everything seemed to be business as usual. Braeden was still wearing his halo and wings. His A.B.L. lit up and he heard the now familiar P.A. voice say, *"Welcome back, my son. Please come to my office. The time has come for you to receive your last power from me, after you tell me what occupation you have decided upon."*

Aleona looked over at Braeden and said, "You heard the man. Get! Oh, wait! What *did* you finally decide on as your occupation?"

Braeden smiled and said, "I'll tell you when I come

back from God's office." He flashed in a burst of colors and light, and suddenly, *he* was a small ball of light.

End of Book 1.

Stay Tuned for Book II and Book III!

Visit the official website at: http://angel.academy/ Register for updates!

(.academy is a new domain extension)

Angel Academy — Book 2

Guardians and Cupids

Chapter 1 -

Twenty years ago...

Off in another galaxy, far, far away, there is a ruckus and a stir in a place called "Oz." Many different individuals live here, in a magical land. An innocent little water fairy has awoken after a very, very long slumber. She sleeps tucked away in a hollow, safe from harm. Her doorway is covered in tulip flowers and small drops of dew.

She yawns and says, "Who's there?"

"It's me, Ivana, it's Edwin."

"Edwin!" she cries out, "It can't be! What are you doing here? How did you get here? How long have I been asleep?"

"Ivana, calm down, I will tell you everything. First of all, I think I've located Jessica. Second, it has been five hundred years and you are being released from your prison as a water fairy."

She sat up, rubbed her eyes, and said, "When will I change back to an angel?"

He whispered, "You will never be an angel again, and you don't have your Angel Bracelet anymore. Ivana, you fell. Fallen angels are borderline demons. You won't be welcomed back into the angel world. You are going to have to hide. But I have a plan... if you help me.

"Three hundred years ago I found the lost Angel Bracelet, and I hid it on a remote, hidden planet called Cybertron. It has now fallen into the hands of machines that have come to life. It would take an army to defeat them. In order to get it back, we need to get the Cracken from Atlantis. It's the only thing that can take on these metal monsters."

She replied back, "Dragon armor is also invincible. If we had some dragons, it would be to our advantage."

"Excellent idea. I never thought of using dragons in our assault," he said.

He took a step back. Ivana started changing shape. She was five inches one second, and then the size of a young child. She did not look like an angel or a water fairy.

"What happened to me?" she cried out.

"I don't know, Ivana, I'm not sure what you are now. I have never been witness to such a punishment," he said, "but if I'm not mistaken, you look very much like an Elf."

Up Next

YOU HAVE JUST READ BOOK 1 OF ANGEL ACADEMY
— THE *NEXT* NEW YORK TIMES & AMAZON
WORLDWIDE BEST SELLER.

Official Release date:

November 18, 2014
Paperback 1st Edition – Amazon.com
Barnes & Noble, Hasting Entertainment

E-book
Amazon.com – Amazon Kindle
Smashwords.com – Barnes & Noble Nook, Apple
iBook, Kobo, Adobe pdf $9.99

December 16, 2014
Limited Edition, 100,000 copies (10,000 already
reserved)
Leather hardbound
Signed Autographed Copy by Author
$99.99

June 2, 2015

All Ebooks go on sale for $4.99

Hardbound version of the book will be available for $29.95

IN THE UPCOMING BOOKS DISCOVER ...

- Who *was* Braeden?
- A deadly battle continues with Morgan & Skye
- What happens to Edwin?
- Why was Morgan investigated in Internal Affairs?
- Who are the Fallen Angels?
- Purgatory and beyond the grave
- Bruce the Angel of ___ ?
- Queen Andromeda Hostage
- Terrorist activity spells doom for ...
- Missing Herald of Atlantis
- The stolen Cupid red ruby heart
- The Nathan, Lucille, and Delilah story continues
- Jack the Demon of Fear

And Much More!

BOOK 2 – GUARDIAN ANGELS – EARTHBOUND

BOOK 3 – CUPID – FOR LOVE & WAR

Follow on Twitter: @aaronmstephens
Facebook.com/officialangelacademy
Facebook.com/officialaaronmstephens
Pinterest.com/aaronmstephens
Website: http://angel.academy/
Author Website: www.aaronmstephens.com

For the latest updates on the book and more!

About The Author

Aaron M. Stephens, M.B.A.

Aaron has spent the majority of his life as a role model, professor, teacher, and guide. He believes in a heart-centered approach to life, using his heart instead of his head to make decisions. He was born under a full moon in South Vietnam. War and terror seized his country, and he and his identical twin brother were adopted into an Army family. His birth father from Vietnam was the youngest of seven boys. Aaron is the 7th son, and his brother is the 8th. It is extremely rare for one to be the 7th son of a 7th son. Less than ten have been identified in the world. At a very young age he was identified as gifted, and could pick up new skills simply by watching others. He was always a straight "A" student and excelled in many areas. Children and animals have always been very fond of Aaron, due to his kind, warm energy.

As a young child he always had a voracious appetite

for books. With incredible reading speed he would devour books in an afternoon. As a child he realized that life was not so adventurous, and he would turn to books to escape into someone else's world, at least temporarily. After reading thousands of other authors' works and styles, he found himself very critical of others' work, and wanted to write something really good, in a literal sense, and as his contribution to society and the world. When it came to creating *Angel Academy* he thought of the stories he had read as a child, and asked himself, what made them so special? The answer was so simple it was staring him in the face. Children of all ages want a magical place where they can live, even if just for an hour at a time.

Aaron has a Bachelor's Degree in Marketing from the University of Nebraska, Kearney. He also holds a Master's Degree in Business Administration, Human Resources/Relationships. Corporate highlights include Director of Marketing, Social Media Director, Product Manager, Director of Web Design, Webmaster, Human Resource Manager, Sales, Trainer, Customer Service, plus many more. He has been published in numerous trade journals, newsletters, and online blogs.

The author was raised in Kearney Nebraska and now resides in Denver, Colorado. When he is not writing books, he is busy designing websites for small business owners and other authors. You can read more of his thoughts on his personal blog at: www.aaronsafterthoughts.com or www.aaronmstephens.com. He designed and created the website for http://Angel.Academy/. He enjoys fantasy fiction, science fiction, and has been an avid comic book reader since he was a young child.

Book Order Form

CHECKS PAYABLE TO: - PHOTOCOPY THIS FORM -

Aaron Stephens
3758 E. 104th Ave. Suite 83
Thornton, CO 80233-4434

Shipping Address:

Contact Name:_____

Organization (if applicable):_____

Address:_____ City: _____

State: ____ Zip/Postal:_____

Daytime Phone: _____
Email: _____

Angel Academy, Book 1, paperback version

Please indicate quantity: ____ books at retail price of $19.95

____ books ($19.95 x __ = $____)
____ books with wholesale discount ($19.95 x .__
X__ = $____)
Colorado Sales Tax 7.50% $_____

Shipping & Handling: $ _____
Total: $_____

If you have a _UPS or _FEDEX account number you may bill your shipping. Please indicate your preferred method of transport and time expectations.

Please indicate how quickly you want your order: _ Ground _ Next Day _ Overnight

Account Number: _____
Authorized Agent Name: _____

If paying with a credit card _ Visa _ MC

Signature: _____

Billing Address: _____

Credit Card Number: _____ exp:____

Amount to be charged, including shipping:$____

Wholesale Book Discount Chart:

```
1 book - 0%
2-10 books - 10%
11-20 book - 20%
21-30 books - 30%
31-40 books - 40%
50 -9,999 books - 50%
10,000 or more 60%
```

Shipping and Handling

$3 per book U.S.A, $2 each additional book • $15 per book International, $10 each additional

Phone: 720-837-1088   Fax: 413-235-0641
Email: requests@aaronmstephens.com

(Church's, non-profit and out of state do not pay sales tax. Colorado Residents pay 7.50% Please include your tax exempt information.

\# _____